TAKEDOWN

Also by Allison van Diepen

STREET PHARM

SNITCH

RAVEN

TAKEDOWN

Allison van Diepen

SIMON PULSE

New York   London   Toronto   Sydney   New Delhi

SIMON PULSE

An imprint of Simon & Schuster Children's Publishing Division

1230 Avenue of the Americas, New York, NY 10020

First Simon Pulse edition September 2013

Copyright © 2013 by Allison van Diepen

For information about special discounts for bulk purchases, please contact Simon & Schuster Special Sales at 1-866-506-1949 or business@simonandschuster.com.

The Simon & Schuster Speakers Bureau can bring authors to your live event. For more information or to book an event contact the Simon & Schuster Speakers Bureau at 1-866-248-3049 or visit our website at www.simonspeakers.com.

Designed by Angela Goddard

The text of this book was set in Adobe Caslon Pro.

Manufactured in the United States of America

2 4 6 8 10 9 7 5 3 1

Library of Congress Cataloging-in-Publication Data

Van Diepen, Allison.

Takedown / Allison van Diepen. — 1st Simon Pulse ed.

p. cm.

Summary: After years in "juvie," Darren cooperates with the police to infiltrate a drug ring to settle a vendetta, but sweet, innocent Jessica is now in his life, so when a deadly turf war erupts, Darren must protect not only his own life, but Jessica's as well.

ISBN 978-1-4424-6311-0 (hc)

[1. Drug traffic—Fiction. 2. Vendetta—Fiction. 3. Criminal investigation—Fiction. 4. African Americans—Fiction.] I. Title.

PZ7.V28526Tak 2013

[Fic]—dc23

2012039237

ISBN 978-1-4424-6312-7 (pbk)

ISBN 978-1-4424-6313-4 (eBook)

For the teachers and librarians who champion my books.

And for the readers who wanted more. This is for you.

THE DEAL

I slipped back into the alley and whispered into my cell, "It's on. Pup's approaching the car."

Seconds ticked by. I watched Pup slide into his shiny black Mazda. Bass thumped inside. If the cops didn't pounce soon, they'd lose him. That better not happen. I'd spent weeks tracking his movements in preparation for this. His car was definitely full of Diamond Dust and who knows what else.

Sirens wailed, and three cop cars streaked in from all sides. Pup slammed on the gas, ramming one of them. He flung open his door and started to run, but they were on him in seconds.

Pup put up an impressive fight, but it only got him zapped by a Taser. Finally they cuffed him and shoved him into the back of a cruiser. Off he went.

I smiled. Seeing Pup get arrested was a pleasure. He was a key player in Diamond Tony Walker's operation. Cruel and unusual was his thing. That's how he got his name—short for Sick Puppy.

Pulling my hood forward, I walked out of the alley and crossed the street, avoiding the security cameras around the all-night deli. Everybody knew those cameras didn't miss a thing. If Diamond Tony suspected a snitch, he'd get the tapes. He could have anything he wanted in this neighborhood.

I wasn't going to get sloppy. A sloppy informant is a dead informant.

Home was four blocks away. It was late and freezing cold, so everybody was staying inside. Even the drug fiends had found warm places to huddle.

When I got to my building, I saw two homeless guys slumped in between the front doors. They were probably too high to notice me, but I couldn't risk it.

I circled around back and scaled the fire escape. It was loose in several places and clanked against the building as I went up three floors. Climbing into my bedroom, I kicked off my shoes, threw my jacket over a chair, and stretched out on the bed. I rubbed my hands together to warm them up. My heart was beating fast, the way it always did when I was creeping. Creeping and peeping, the kind of thing that could get me killed any day of the week.

I was four months out of juvie and a lot deeper into the game than before I went in. But I had to work for Diamond Tony if I was going to bring him down. I had a mission—and nothing was going to get in my way.

Pup's arrest tonight was just the beginning.

THE STOP

I stood at the bus stop the next morning, the wind biting my ears. Trey was standing beside me, running his mouth. I'd known him forever. Everybody had. He knew every bus route and where it went and would go on about it nonstop.

November was the ugliest time of year in the Jane and Finch projects. The trees were like skeletons, the grass dead and brown. It was a concrete jungle with huge high-rises that loom over you like Big Brother. I hated how bare it all looked. Reminded me of the cell blocks of juvie. I wished winter would come and cover the place with snow.

Trey carried a paper bag—his daily bacon, egg, and cheese

sandwich made a big splotch of grease at the bottom. Me, I never ate before first period. Instead I sipped my morning drink: coffee mixed with hot chocolate. Today I ordered three-quarters coffee. I hadn't slept much. I was too wired from last night. Detective Prescott had called soon after I got home to tell me how it all went down. Pup's car had been loaded with drugs and weapons. I was glad, but when I finally fell asleep, my dreams were full of guns, shouting, and running. I was always having dreams like that.

Trey's whine interrupted my thoughts. "The forty-seven again! It's only supposed to show up every twelve minutes. It's been eight minutes. The driver must be smoking weed."

"More like crack," I said. "Weed would slow him down."

He didn't get the joke. "Our bus better be on time. I've got a test."

"Chill, T. It'll be here."

"I need to ace this one, so I don't want to start late. How are your grades?"

"Okay." I had a B average so far, but I was determined to crank it up to the next level. Too bad juvie had left me way behind. I should be a senior, but I was taking tenth- and eleventh-grade classes.

"You've only been absent twice. You're better than you used to be. Remember the time you missed ten days in one month?"

I couldn't help but smile. "Actually, I don't remember, T."

Peeps at school was always calling Trey Ass-Burger because he had autism, the type that made you really smart.

Before he could say more, Biggie and Smalls came up to us. Also known as BJ and Lex, they'd been best friends practically since birth, mostly because they'd both grown up in the 15 high-rise. They were a weird-looking pair since Biggie was stocky and over six feet tall, and Smalls was so short and scrawny, people often mistook him for a twelve-year-old. Smalls was the one with the mouth, though. I'd known these guys for years, and before I went to juvie, we used to hang out. Not anymore. I'd lost too much time to be wasting it with guys who did nothing but smoke up and play video games. They were never gonna get out of the projects, and if I spent too much time with them, I wouldn't either.

"You hear Pup got arrested last night?" Smalls's voice went all high like a girl. "Our man Diamond Tony's gonna be pissed!"

I knew a few smart people, and Smalls wasn't one of them. There were a lot of guys like him in Jane and Finch. He was against everything—authority, common sense, probably even good nutrition. He thought the news was all propaganda made up by The Man. Truth was, he was as much of a follower as anyone else. He actually believed the real heroes were people like Diamond Tony, who weren't scared of the cops and who didn't follow society's rules or the Ten Commandments. Smalls was a damned fool.

While we waited for the bus, the guys shared stories about Pup and all the sick shit he'd done. Pup was Tony's goon, and torture was his MO. He didn't torture to extract information, though. He did it because he enjoyed it.

The bus finally came, and we had to push our way on. Biggie and I stood on the bottom step and squeezed up against a fat guy so the driver could close the door. The bus ride took forever. Each time it stopped, I had to get off to let people exit, then fight to get back on. A short, wrinkled lady dressed in black elbowed past me. Same thing every day with that one. It was like being old gave her the right to do whatever she wanted.

Finally the bus dropped us off in front of the school. Smalls and I went to our first class, history. *Tenth-grade* history. Smalls's only excuse was that he was lazy. I didn't sit with him because I didn't want the teacher to think I was lazy too. Smalls thought I sat at the other end of the classroom to be next to this hot chick Tiara.

When class started, Mr. Monk said, "Clear your desks."

I could have kicked myself. I'd been so focused on the Pup mission that I'd forgotten all about the test.

Shit. I was going to have to do better.

Two classes later, I was in my happy place. The synthesizer pumped a raw beat.

I rapped inside my head:

Hup, hup, brought down the pup
Sick bitch had a free ride
He'll pay on the inside.

The rest of the class was across the room playing instruments, but Mr. Filimino let me do my thing. He knew that violins and trumpets weren't for me, so he was cool with me making beats and writing rhymes.

The music room was a big space that used to be the industrial arts workshop. Mr. Filimino had moved the music classes here because the acoustics were better than in any classroom. I switched the beat, speeding it up.

The King's going down
I'm'a rip off his crown
Smash it under my feet
You'll wanna know the deets
The hood'll finally be free
Like how it used to be
No more terror monarchy.

Making music was the only time I had the flow. I could focus so intensely that hours felt like minutes. I'd stay in the zone until every beat was in place, until every word was perfection.

In juvie, I'd missed making music more than anything. I wasn't allowed to have my keyboard or turntables because they could be used as weapons. As if I'd ruin my expensive equipment just to whack somebody over the head with it. So all I had was a notebook full of rhymes. I'd repeat the songs over and over so I wouldn't forget the tunes. Finally I got approval to have an old handheld tape recorder.

My plan was to go to Ryerson University. Lots of music producers went there. After that, me and my friend from juvie, White Chris, were going to start our own record label, Juvenile Records. Chris knew how to drop a rhyme and, like me, had a head for business. Ryerson didn't just want good audition tapes—they wanted good grades and recommendation letters, too. Luckily, I could count on Mr. Filimino to give me a rec when the time came. He was the one teacher who didn't seem to hold my record against me.

The bell rang for lunch period. Most of the class left, but a few stayed behind to watch me play. I hardly knew them, since they were two years younger than me. Eventually it was just me and Ricky, a skinny kid with too many zits and not enough deodorant.

"Can I try out some lyrics?" he asked.

"Go for it."

He gave a nervous cough as I slowed down the beat. Then he started. "I don't need a pill/To make this beat ill/Sit back and hold still/My lyrics gonna thrill."

"Sick," I said. Pretty basic beginner lyrics, but he had rhythm.

"I want to learn all this," he said, touching the dials.

"Filimino will let you use it at lunchtime. If he trusts you."

"Yeah?" I could see the question in his eyes. *Filimino trusts you?*

"He knows I'd never steal shit this old. I got better stuff at home."
Ricky grinned.

"If you want to stay, go ask him." Filimino was at the other end
of the room stacking chairs.

He hesitated. "Wait, can you show me how to get that beat again?"

"Sure."

As I showed him, I had the feeling I was being watched. I
glanced up. Some girls stood in the doorway.

One of them was Jessica Thomas. She was in economics with
me—one of my three eleventh-grade classes. Some people said
Jessica looked like Rihanna, but I thought she was way prettier.
They say the only reason she wasn't a model was that she was too
short, maybe five two or three. She had flawless skin, full glossy
lips, and big brown eyes that could make you forget your name.
Yeah, thoughts of Jessica Thomas kept me company while I was
in juvie.

I turned back to Ricky. "You good to go?"

"Yeah, thanks."

I grabbed my books and headed for the door. The girls stepped
out of my way, but Jessica said, "Hey, Darren."

She had a shy look in her eyes. I wasn't sure if I bought it. This was Jessica Thomas, after all. Sometimes guys called her Jessica *Bing* because of the effect her sweet curves could have on your imagination. But she was known as a good girl. She had this cheerful, fresh thing about her that was different from most girls.

"Hi," I said, and kept on walking. I heard them squeal behind me.

The fact was, a lot of girls were noticing me lately. I wasn't the gangly freshman who'd left for juvie more than two years ago—I'd worked out daily while I was locked up. And now that I was on Diamond Tony's payroll, I could finally afford to wear the hottest brands and real bling around my neck.

The only thing the girls admired more than the clothes was my new street cred. Days after leaving juvie, I was back on the streets as a full-fledged dealer. They probably thought that took balls.

They had no clue.

INFORMER

That afternoon I sat with Detective Prescott at a café on Bay Street. We were in the Financial District, where white-collared rich guys traded stocks. The place was usually packed with businesspeople lined up for the overpriced salad bar, but now it was mostly empty. If you saw us, you'd think we were father and son. Maybe teacher and student.

Not cop and informant.

As a rule, I didn't like cops. I'd seen too many people roughed up, harassed, and humiliated. Instead of the motto "To serve and protect" it should be "Because I can." But Prescott was all right. He treated me with respect and even talked about personal stuff, like how his five-month-old twins were up all night fussing. I knew it could be a strategy—make a personal connection to keep your informant loyal—but I didn't care.

Prescott guzzled a coffee, stuffed in a brownie, and talked all at the same time. He was in his late thirties, five ten, and built like a weight lifter who'd gone soft. Something about him being black made me like him more . . . and less. Black cops acted like they were on your side, like they *knew* how it was. Most white cops didn't even pretend. But black cops were also criticized for arresting their brothers to get ahead.

I guess that was something Prescott and I had in common. A black cop was a traitor, and so was I.

"This morning I was so tired, I literally fell asleep while I was shaving," he said, pointing to a cut on his chin.

"Jeez."

"Did you see the press conference the other day?"

"No."

"Sorry, I should've phoned you. We called it to show off all the goodies we got from Pup's arrest. Crack, guns, the whole deal. You should've seen me, spiffy in my blues."

I didn't like the sound of it. "Seriously? You went bragging on TV?"

"It's good PR. We do it whenever we have a major bust, to show we're not screwing around all day. I told the reporters it took

countless hours of painstaking police work to make it happen."
He winked. "'Course, I couldn't mention my secret weapon."

Thank God for that. If Prescott had let it slip that he had someone on the inside, Tony would go head-hunting. And he wouldn't
stop until he found the snitch. "You and the chief can go ahead and
soak up the glory. I sure as hell don't want it."

"I hear you. Now, back to business. Tony's gotta be bringing
in a shitload of cocaine to make the Diamond Dust. How do you
think he's shipping it?"

"I can only guess. Lots of delivery trucks around."

He tugged his earlobe and stared off into space. Prescott always
did that when he was thinking. "How about you find out for me?"

"I'll do what I can, but I can't promise anything. I have to be
careful not to blow my cover."

"Fair enough. You're a clever kid, Darren. That was some nice
work you did the other night. Because of you, we got all we need
on Owen Bradford."

He must have been talking about Pup.

"We hope to have Bradford off the streets for ten years. He's
got a long rap sheet, so that should push the judge to give him the
max. We think he's responsible for three murders carried out by
Tony Walker's gang. Can't prove it, though."

The murders weren't news to me. Word on the street was that

Pup had taken out Pistol, the leader of the South Side Bloods, a few months back. And that he'd really messed up a couple of guys from Hamilton who tried to cut a deal with Tony's suppliers.

"I dropped something," Prescott said, a gleam in his eye.

I ducked to find the paper bag under the table. Without looking inside, I shoved it in my knapsack.

"There's a bonus fifty in there from me. You're putting yourself at risk for a good cause, Darren. And if I make another bust like that one, I may be in line for a promotion." He grinned. "Don't spend it all in one place, now."

I glanced at my watch. "I gotta be somewhere. Are we done?"

Prescott nodded. "Catch ya later."

Grabbing my knapsack, I left the café and ran to the subway station. When I got to the platform, there was a train waiting, and I slipped in right before the doors shut. Even better, I snagged the last seat.

I thought about the cash in my knapsack, probably one fifty, including Prescott's bonus. I'd give some of it to Mom to help with the bills, and the rest would go straight into the bank to save for college.

The train stopped and a flood of people came on. A thirty-something lady glared at me like I should give up my seat, but unless she was going to tell me she was pregnant, I wasn't moving. Not my fault her feet hurt from those heels.

I checked my watch: 3:36. Usually I picked up my brother by 3:30. He'd be wondering where I was. Not that he can tell time, but he knows I always pick him up after nap.

By 3:50, I was there. Home care was supposed to be homey, but this one wasn't. Noreen took care of six kids, sometimes more if a neighbor needed a last-minute babysitter. I could tell that Kiki wasn't getting much attention. Whenever I got there, he was snotty nosed with a wet diaper.

I went in, and there he was, building a perfect tower of blocks. Kiki was only two, but you could already tell he was smart. He was good at putting things together, figuring out how they worked. He ran up to me and hurled himself into my arms. I hoisted him up and spun him around like a superhero. His arms circled my neck, and he gave me a look that said, "Where the hell you been?"

"Sorry I'm late, Kiki."

His answer was a wet slobber on my cheek.

I got his gear on. "Thanks, Noreen," I said, and Kiki waved bye-bye.

Noreen was trying to pull apart two screaming toddlers. "Bye, Kiki!"

In the hallway, I was about to put him down, but he clung to my neck and tightened his legs around me, so I kept holding him. "All right. I was late, so you call the shots today. What's my name, again?"

"Da-win."

"What's your name?"

"HeeHee." He hadn't mastered the K sound yet.

The projects were pretty quiet because it had started to rain. I pulled Kiki's hat down over his ears. "I know what you're thinking, little bro. You're wondering why you gotta grow up in such an ugly-ass place. Gimme eight years. By the time you're ten, I'll have you set up someplace nice. I promise."

We reached our building, and I climbed the stairs, which was faster than waiting for an elevator. I held him with one arm while keying the lock, then washed his hands, changed his diaper, and put on some cartoons. There was a box of Goldfish crackers in the cupboard, but it was empty. I never understood why Mom put empty stuff back in the cupboards—maybe because the cupboard was closer than the garbage can.

I checked for Cheerios, but there were only Bran Flakes, and I knew Kiki wouldn't go for them. I found a protein bar in my knapsack and cut it into little pieces, then gave it to him in his favorite Spider-Man bowl. At the first bite of chocolate, he was happy. I figured the protein would be good for him, especially since we were also out of milk.

I wrote a note for Mom with a list of things we needed and left it on the table with some money. It amazed me that my family had survived while I was in juvie, but I guess Tasha had picked up the slack. It wasn't that Mom didn't make money—she did okay as a dental receptionist—but she spent it all wrong. Too much takeout, too many beauty products.

At least Kiki had Tasha and me. We'd just had Mom. I couldn't even remember my dad. He died when I was eight months old on a peacekeeping mission to Bosnia. I only had one picture of him. He was wearing his military fatigues and a blue peacekeeper's cap. He looked strong and intelligent. A modern-day hero, the way I saw it. Sometimes I wondered how my life would've been different if he were alive. Maybe I wouldn't have ended up in juvie. But then, if Dad had been around, there wouldn't be a Kiki.

"Hey," Tasha said when she walked in the door a while later. She slung her wet jacket over a chair and went right over to Kiki. "Where's my hug, sweetie?"

He complied without taking his eyes off the TV.

"You gave him a chocolate bar for snack? Seriously?"

I didn't look up from my magazine. "It's a protein bar."

"There's probably way too much protein in it for him. What if it makes him sick?"

"I've never heard of protein making you sick. There's nothing else to eat anyway."

"You could've taken him to the store."

"It's raining. Maybe you didn't notice."

She sighed loudly. I could never do anything right.

Tasha always gave me a hard time. When we were kids, she'd teased me and grabbed my toys and pushed me in the dirt. But she'd also stood up for me when bigger kids wanted to knock me around.

If she'd had a soft spot for me back then, she didn't anymore. When I got charged with dealing, she called me every nasty name in the book. She told me it was my fault Mom went into labor early with Kiki, not pregnancy diabetes like Mom said. And she visited me every month to tell me how hard it was at home with the baby and with Mom struggling to pay the bills.

Tasha sat down across from me, opened her knapsack, and pulled out a textbook. That was my cue. "Time to go to work," I said.

"Whatever."

I stood up. "Is there something you want to say?"

She knew I was dealing. So did Mom. It was another reason for Tasha to look down on me, but she never said anything. And I knew why.

She glanced at the money on the table.

"Later," I said.

EVIL

Some people say that no one is born evil—that life makes you that way.

But I knew that wasn't true. Plenty of people got fucked over by life, beaten into the ground, and spit on. But they didn't end up like Diamond Tony.

All I wanted this morning was my choco-latte and a quick bus to school. Instead I got a crime scene right in the middle of the projects.

Somebody shoved past me to get closer. I stepped back, away from the crowd, away from the stench. I'd caught a glimpse of the body and the bloodstained ground and didn't want to see more.

Everybody was saying that it was Rico, Pup's brother. And that Tony had done the job himself.

A light-skinned girl was screaming. Must be Rico's girlfriend. She ran toward the body, but her friends tried to pull her back. Finally the crowd parted to let her get closer, and she collapsed, shrieking. Her friends picked her up and dragged her away. Smart friends. If she stuck around the crime scene too long, she might say or do something that would put her on Tony's hit list.

People in the crowd kept asking why. Had Rico been planning to rat on Tony to get Pup a lighter sentence? Or was it Tony's way of telling Pup to keep quiet or the rest of his family would die? I wanted to shout at them that it didn't even matter. Tony was sending a message to the whole neighborhood. *Don't talk. Be afraid. Don't think I won't.*

The crowd suddenly hushed. A group of guys were crossing the projects ten yards away. It was Diamond Tony and his entourage.

They say killers like to hang out by their crime scenes. I guess it's true. From a distance, Tony could be any random guy in a black bomber jacket and Jays cap, but the sunglasses gave him away. He wore them whenever he was outside, whether it was sunny or gray, morning or night. Tony waved at the crowd like a celebrity greeting his fans.

Evil.

THE KID

When I was fifteen, I got recruited as a lookout. That's how it started.

I felt honored and bragged about it to my friends. I got paid, sure, but I'd have done it for free, just for the status of being a part of Diamond Tony's operation.

I didn't know back then what Diamond Tony was made of. All I knew was that he was the most notorious kingpin Toronto had ever seen.

It was all good for a few weeks. I had as much MPR—money, power, and respect—as a kid could hope for. Then one day, while a deal was going down, the cops descended on us from every direction. One of Tony's guys shoved a package into my hand. "You know the code." We ran off in different directions, but I didn't get far before the police tackled me.

In the cruiser, I had this jittery feeling. I knew the code: Don't snitch. If I named names, I'd pay the price. My family would too.

They put me in a white room that was as small as a prison cell. There was a table attached to the floor and three chairs. Two detectives, a skinny white guy and a short, Jennifer-Lopez-plus-thirty-pounds, came in to interrogate me.

Skinny paced around the table. "Why don't you make this easy on yourself and tell us who those drugs belong to?"

"I'm waiting for my lawyer." Everybody knew that Diamond Tony had a fancy-ass lawyer who represented his people. I hoped he'd send him soon.

Skinny flattened his palms on the table and leaned toward me. "Why would you need a lawyer?" I jerked my head back at his coffee breath. "The crack isn't yours, is it?"

I didn't answer.

That's when J.Lo started in on me. "All you need to do is tell us who gave you the drugs and what they asked you to do."

"No one and nothing, ma'am."

Skinny raked a hand across his bad comb-over. "How would a kid like you get half a kilo of crack in the middle of Walker territory?"

Half a kilo? Shit. I glanced at the door, wishing Diamond Tony's lawyer would hurry the hell up.

J.Lo pulled a chair up next to me and gave me a motherly look. "You can tell us the truth, Darren. That's what'll get you out of this."

I forced a laugh. It wasn't a mother I needed—it was Witness Protection.

She might've guessed my thoughts, because she said, "If you're willing to talk, we can keep a close eye on you and your family."

Yeah, like a cruiser driving by a couple of times a day would protect us if I snitched.

"Half a kilo is serious, Darren," she said. "You could spend several years in juvie, and then you could serve the remainder of your time in an adult prison. Is that worth it to you?"

I didn't answer. My stomach clenched, and it was all I could do not to throw up. I wanted to run away. Pretend none of this was happening.

But it was.

The Mission

Before I left juvie
I told the cops I had a plan

TAKEDOWN

To bring down Diamond Tony
Number-one wanted man
They gave me some green, an ID number, and
   a phone
It was better than nothing
I would've done it on my own.

IN THE BIZ

We got a problem on our hands," Vinny said, looking around at his dealers. It was Friday at five, and we'd been called to an emergency meeting. "South Side Bloods are moving in on us."

We all went quiet as we took in the news. Vinny was our lieutenant, the guy who connected us to Tony's operation. The moment I'd heard about the meeting, I knew something was up. Though Vinny was in charge of six dealers, I'd rarely been in the same room with the others.

Vinny was a former foster kid. His face had scars of a rough life, the kind that all the money in the world couldn't erase. He was probably twenty-two, twenty-three, but half his teeth had silver caps, with a gold one at the front. I'd heard that Diamond Tony's operation snatched him up young and raised him as their own. Tony's choices were never random. Vinny was smart, but not so smart he'd ever question Tony. And Vinny was loyal—how could you not be when you got pulled from the gutter? Even if he came off as cocky, that didn't bother anyone. You could tell he was trying so hard to be somebody.

Vinny's town house was full of classy furniture and high-tech gadgets, but we were down in his basement for the meeting, which had a musty smell and saggy old couches.

"The Bloods ain't gonna take away our business," T-Bone said, waving his hand like he was swatting at a fly. "Our fiends know we got the raw product. What they got is weak."

Vinny shook his head. "Not anymore. They got good shit now. Some are saying it's better than ours. And they been dropping their prices to undercut us."

I was surprised Vinny was admitting that another operation could have a product as potent as Diamond Dust. It was a crack-cocaine so pure, so gleaming white, that once you got hooked, you could never be satisfied with anything else. Tony had managed to do what every businessman dreamed of. He'd created a product that people literally couldn't live without.

"If I see one of their dealers in our territory, I'll take him out." Albert put a hand to his side, showing he was strapped. "DT fought hard for his territory. Brothers died for this. We ain't giving up a single corner."

"Don't go shooting anybody unless you have to, hear me?" Vinny said. "The cops are watching us. That's how Pup got caught. DT says we have to go dark for a while, which means no shoot-outs."

That didn't mean no *shooting*, just not in public. Diamond Tony didn't do diplomacy.

"So what am I supposed to do when I see the Bloods around?" Albert demanded.

"Ask them to kindly move along," Cam said in an old-lady voice, and we all laughed.

Cam was my dealing partner. We'd grown up together in the neighborhood, so I was glad when Vinny had put us together. Cam was a dropout and a heavy weed smoker with a talent for imitating people. Even when he mimicked the neighborhood assholes, they were too impressed to get pissed off. He had a huge mop of red hair and the words "Thug Life" tattooed on his arm—the only white guy I knew with a tattoo like that.

Cam's comment might've made us laugh, but like everybody else, he was waiting for an answer to Albert's question.

Vinny didn't seem to have one. "Don't do shit without calling me, a'ight? I gotta check everything with DT. He's counting on his soldiers to keep it locked. Can y'all handle that?"

Everybody nodded. Their chests puffed out. They liked being Diamond Tony Walker's street soldiers. They liked working for a legend.

The guys started talking about how weak the South Side Bloods were, but I was only half listening. The Bloods were ballsy to make a play for Diamond Tony's territory. It must be their new leader, Andre. He'd been Pistol's top lieutenant and had taken over after Pistol died. Andre was known for being calculating and fearless—he'd have to be to take on Tony. And he had more lives than a cat. Rumor had it he'd been shot five different times.

I bet Andre's play for Walker territory was more than just business. It was revenge for Pistol's murder. I was sure that a lot of people secretly wanted to see Diamond Tony go down, but they didn't have the courage to do anything about it.

The thought made me smile. I was doing some *real* community service.

Vinny brought us pizza and wings but told us to eat fast so we could get to our corners. It was incredible how happy the guys were when they saw the spread. For all the money we made for Tony, we should've been given cars, not pizza and wings.

By six we were wiping our hands and getting up from the

saggy couches. When we headed upstairs, there were some guys in the living room.

One of them was Diamond Tony.

My skin prickled. I'd never seen him up close and never without his sunglasses. I glanced away quickly, but not before I caught a glimpse of his eyes. They were dead, glassy. The eyes of a sociopath. I wondered if that was why he always wore sunglasses—so people wouldn't see who he really was.

He didn't look like the kingpins you saw on TV. He didn't dress to get attention. He always wore a clean, crisp outfit. Tonight, it was white and blue Enyce with shoes that were brand-new. If you looked closely, you saw the signs of wealth: the diamond in his ear, the diamond-studded infinity symbol around his neck. Some people thought that's how he got his name. But when you saw Diamond Dust sparkle in the sunlight, you knew that's where it came from.

There were two huge guys with him, obviously his security, and two of his executives, Marcus and Donut. Marcus gave off this cold, remote vibe that reminded me of a robot. Programmed to do whatever Tony wanted, no doubt.

Vinny walked into the living room and gestured for us to follow. "Here they are."

Diamond Tony got up. We all stood up straighter, like military recruits waiting for inspection. He looked us over, one by one, and when he got to me, he paused thoughtfully. "Darren Lewis," he said.

Blood rushed in my ears. *Is he onto me?*

"Soldier," he said, and clapped a hand on my shoulder before moving on to the next guy. I was sure I was pitted with sweat.

After he'd looked over the last guy, Diamond Tony sat back down. "You told them?" he asked Vinny.

"I told them. You got solid soldiers here, Tony. They're gonna make you proud."

Tony didn't take his eyes off us. "Of course they will." In true Diamond style, it was both a vote of confidence and a threat.

Then Vinny sent us out into the night.

ZOMBIES

Cam and I went to our corner in front of the 17 high-rise. It took a while for my pulse to slow down. How had Tony recognized me? We'd never actually met. I'd seen him a few times, but I hadn't thought he'd noticed me.

Obviously I was wrong about that.

Maybe he didn't stay as far in the background as I imagined. Who knew how many times he'd driven by our corner, watching through some tinted-windowed SUV?

I didn't like it.

When I was fifteen, I would've been excited that Diamond Tony knew who I was. But I wasn't a dumb kid anymore. Now

I knew the game he was playing, and I saw right through him.

I just hoped he couldn't see through me.

Tonight the fiends were out in full force. Reminded me of a zombie movie. They were slow but jittery, dragging themselves toward us. Sometimes I had to remind myself that they weren't the walking dead.

Growing up in the projects, I knew what addiction looked like. But selling on the corner night after night really brought the ugly home. I saw normal people become strung-out fiends in a matter of weeks.

The creepiest zombie was this guy called the Vet. He wore a raggedy green army jacket and told everybody he'd fought in Afghanistan. He was skinny as hell, with sunken eyes and sores.

The Vet came up to me with mostly change from panhandling. I counted it and put it in my pocket, then gave Cam the signal and he supplied him. We watched the Vet shuffle away. Cam pulled a face. I could tell the Vet freaked him out too.

"You going to the party later?" Cam asked me.

"Yeah." Smalls had been talking about his party all week, so I figured I'd go.

"Tell your sister to come," Cam said with a grin. "I'm aching to get laid."

"She'd help you out, but she'd need a gas mask to put up with your stank."

Cam laughed.

After we did the final exchange of the night with Vinny, we headed to the party. The apartment was jammed with people. It was dark, lit only with purple lightbulbs, and the air reeked of weed and cognac cigarillos.

Cam saw a pothead friend and said, "Catch ya later." Then he headed for one of the bedrooms. I grabbed a bottle of Scotch off the dining room table. White Chris always said it was your choice of liquor that separated the men from the boys. Too bad I had to drink it from a red plastic cup.

A cute Vietnamese girl caught my eye, and I smiled at her. She smiled back, then whispered something to her friend, who seemed to be urging her to approach me. I wanted to tell her friend not to rush it. I hadn't scoped the whole place yet.

I made my way to the kitchen, where a bunch of people were talking about last night's game. Vinny was already there, no surprise. He showed up anywhere that people paid attention to him, even if it was a party of mostly high school kids. Maybe he was looking for a new girl. Or, if the rumors were true, two or three girls.

Vinny saw me and gave a shout-out. I raised my cup to him.

Eventually I went back to the living room. It was too loud to talk much, so I just stood next to Smalls and we watched the girls dancing.

Then I spotted Jessica sipping from a shot glass. It was too dark to see the look in her eyes when she saw me, but I knew the second she did—something in her posture changed, like she'd suddenly snapped awake. I liked that I had that effect on her.

The music pumped through my veins like a drug. My foot moved forward as if to go to her, but I froze. It wasn't the best time to start something with Jessica. I didn't need anything, or anyone, taking my mind off the game, and school was enough of a distraction.

But the part of me that had been locked up for two years said she was exactly what I needed.

The next thing I knew, I was right in front of Jessica. Her eyes were level with my chest, but she tipped her head up. The makeup on her eyelids sparkled.

She might've said, "Hi," but I could hardly hear anything. The throbbing music had vocals—loud, heavy vocals.

She went on her tiptoes, and I felt her breath in my ear. "I was hoping you'd show up."

I raised a brow. "You wanted to see my dance moves."

Jessica laughed and flipped her hair. She usually straightened it, but tonight it was big and curly. As usual, she smelled like heaven. "You learned some new moves in juvie?"

"Yeah, total dance party. Makes you never want to leave."

Her smile faded. "Everyone was pissed off that you got put

away for so long." I thought she might say more, but then she shrugged. "You've got some partying to make up for."

"I'll need your help for that."

The outside world vanished, and it was just me and her. She did most of the dancing, but she let me move with her. We kept looking at each other and smiling, her eyes the only real light in the darkness.

I had the urge to laugh. Four months out of juvie, and here I was dancing with Jessica Thomas. I couldn't believe it.

I'm not sure when it all ended, but in the early hours of the morning, I dragged myself home with Jessica's number programmed into my phone. And I fell asleep in my clothes, covered in the scent of Jessica.

PERSONAL DEMON

Sunday afternoon I met up with Prescott at the Shanghai Palace in the fancy Yorkville shopping district. I didn't think he had a shift today, but it didn't matter. He was a twenty-four-seven kind of cop.

The restaurant was half-full, and everything inside was red and brassy. There were five dishes of food on the table. He'd already started eating when I got there. Still, it was better than the cookie and iced tea he usually got me.

"I need a favor, Darren," he said, flashing some half-chewed chow mein. "A big one."

"Go on." I loaded up my plate.

Prescott leaned closer, probably more for effect than because he thought anyone was listening. Our table was in the back corner near the kitchen. There was a fly caught between the curtain and the window, buzzing away. I was tempted to squash it.

"They're putting pressure on me, Darren. The chief wants to break the drug trade in this city wide open, and he wants to do it before the election. I need to know how the coke's getting in."

"I'll be watching," I said between bites. "That's all I can promise." The food was tasty. There was actually chicken in the chicken balls, not the mystery meat you got in my neighborhood.

"Any of the executives could be doing the drug runs," he said. "I doubt Tony Walker would trust anyone else with that kind of money. Whoever does it will probably have another guy or two with him for security. Not that it makes a difference. If the Demon's Sons want to take them out, they'll do it."

"The who?"

"Demon's Sons. A biker gang based south of the border. They're Tony's suppliers. They buy coke from their cartel connection in Mexico and ship it all over the U.S. and Canada. If you help me out with this one, I'll give you a grand. How does that sound?"

"I don't do it for the money, you know that. But my hand won't shake when I take the cash."

Prescott laughed and smacked the table. "You could be a cop one day."

Now, that was over the top, even for Prescott. "Yeah, right. With my record."

"Why not? I'd put in a word for you. And by then, I might be another rung or two up the ladder. You never know." He drowned an egg roll in plum sauce and took a few bites. "So. Last time we met, you mentioned delivery trucks. You still think the coke gets in that way?"

"Could be. Or maybe it's shipped up through the port."

Prescott gripped the table. "Specifics, Darren. I need specifics. Not speculation."

"I got you." Guess Prescott really wanted that promotion. This wasn't personal for him, though. Not like for me.

"Walker's got to be laundering the money somehow," Prescott said. "His name isn't connected to any business we can find, but he has to be funneling it through some local businesses. Especially ones that deal with cash, like nail salons, car washes, clubs. Call me with anything you have, Darren. No detail's too small."

"There's something you should know." I swallowed. He definitely wasn't going to like this. "The South Side Bloods have a new leader, Andre. He was Pistol's—"

"I know who Andre is. That sly sonofabitch. We couldn't even convict him on a possession charge, for fuck's sake."

"Well, Andre's making a play for Tony's territory. He must've found a new supplier, because their product is better than it used to be. Maybe better than Diamond Dust."

Prescott rubbed his face, kind of like Kiki did when he was worn out. "That's all we need. A new line into the city. And maybe a turf war. How long before it turns bloody?"

"Don't know. Tony's telling his men to stand down for now. Since Pup got locked up, he's extra worried."

"He should be." Prescott shook his head, like he was trying to shake a bad memory. "I was a beat cop when Walker showed up ten years ago. Seemed like a new body turned up every week. Sometimes it was a rival dealer. Or their girlfriend. Or a kid hit by a stray bullet. It didn't used to be that way, you know. There were always drugs, but it was never this bloody till he came around. There used to be a code, an unwritten rule among the drug dealers to keep the innocents out of the game. But for Walker, no one was off-limits." His stare was intense. "I can't wait to lock him up."

Maybe I was wrong about Prescott. Maybe it was personal for him, too.

MO MONDAY

Monday morning started with another test, but this time, I was ready. My brain was full, and when I saw the questions, I puked everything I knew onto the page.

The classifications of life, according to my bio textbook: *Kingdom, Phylum, Class, Order, Family, Genus, Species*. I had the urge to rewrite it, a classification of life projects-style: *Kingpin, Executives, Lieutenants, Dealers, Ordinary People, Fiends*. But I pushed those thoughts from my mind and focused on the test, flying through all five pages in good time. My memory for detail was solid, especially since I'd become an informant.

When we were finished, we got to leave class early, so I stopped by the music room. Filimino had a prep this period, and I found him behind a mountain of paper.

"Hey, Darren," he said, raising his head. "You want to help me mark some tests?"

"What's in it for me?"

He considered that. "A few hours of pulling your hair out. These freshmen don't listen to a fucking word I say. I'm just going to use the Chinese method."

"What's that?"

"It's where you throw the papers down the stairs and whatever lands farthest gets an A, and so on."

I wasn't sure he was joking. Filimino was one of those teachers who broke all the rules. He bitched. He swore. He was always clashing with our uptight principal, and he once told me he wouldn't have a job if it weren't for the union saving his ass.

"There's an orientation night coming up at Ryerson, if you're interested. You can sign up at the guidance office."

"I'll go next year. I've got plenty of time."

He shrugged. "I thought you might want to check out their equipment. You could always see what George Brown has to offer too."

It was cool that Filimino was thinking about my college options. He was the only adult in my life who actually took the music production thing seriously. Mom thought it was a pointless hobby, not a career.

Filimino knew how it was. He was a musician himself, and had toured all over the world with his band in the nineties. He played guitar and drums and wowed the class with what he could do.

The bell rang, and I headed upstairs to economics. I caught sight of Jessica at her locker and said, "Hi." Her eyes narrowed a bit, but then she said a lukewarm "Hi" back.

I'd promised to call her. I was hoping she'd forget, but who was I kidding? Girls never forget. I'd heard my sister's complaints enough to know that.

I'd actually picked up the phone to call her last night, but then my conscience kicked in. I liked Jessica, and I didn't want to screw her around. I was playing a dangerous game, and if she became my girlfriend, she could be at risk. That scared me.

I hoped our time would come. But it couldn't be now.

Honor

Honor's what it's called
Kids don't know what it means
They wanna make the money
supplyin' all the fiends

Allison van Diepen

You think it's all good
You don't even know it's wrong
Till it hits you in the face
Like a brick in the face
It hits you in the face
Days in juvie sure are long.

THE INVESTMENT

Thursday morning I got lucky. I snagged a seat on the bus, which saved me from getting elbowed by that old lady. Trey sat beside me, rambling on as usual. Smalls and Biggie were in front of us.

"This is the real deal." Biggie caught the sunlight with his shiny new watch and reflected it all over the bus. "You know how many shifts I worked for this? Worth every minute."

Trey wasn't impressed. "If that watch cost three hundred dollars plus tax and you make minimum wage, then you had to work seven shifts to buy it."

Biggie burst out laughing. Trey seemed pleased with himself, as if he'd told an awesome joke.

I didn't think Biggie should've blown all that money on a watch, but at least his money came legit. He'd been working at Artie's Pizza for years. It might've made him fat, but at least it kept him out of trouble.

"You could have gotten a more expensive watch than that," Trey said. This from a guy who was known for his Batman knapsack.

"Oh yeah?" Biggie said. "What kind of watch would *you* get, Bat Boy?"

"That's not what I meant. I've seen you cashing your pay checks at the Cash Stop. It's a waste of money. That's five percent you're throwing away. On a three-hundred-dollar purchase, that's fifteen bucks. If you make three hundred a month, that's one hundred and eighty dollars you're losing a year."

Biggie shrugged. "Yeah, but you go to the bank and they're chargin' for this and that anyway. I like to keep my money where I can see it, you know? Besides, everyone goes there. Even the execs. And when it comes to cash, you know they ain't playing." He pounded fists with Smalls.

"You can get a no-fee student account at the bank on the corner of Finch and Keele," Trey said. "And you can use their bank machine ten times a month for no fee. My sister got an account and saved . . ."

He kept talking, but their eyes glazed over. The guys turned back toward the front of the bus, and I pretended to listen to Trey, but my mind was tripping in another direction.

So the executives went to the Cash Stop. That meant something. It had to.

Diamond Tony wouldn't be paying his guys with checks, that's for sure. If executives went there, they were doing business.

Prescott had said that Diamond Tony would be laundering money through businesses that dealt with large amounts of cash. I couldn't think of a more perfect place than the Cash Stop. Half the neighborhood went there to cash checks, get loans, or send money. Even my mom cashed her checks there when she couldn't be bothered waiting at the bank.

I would have to check it out. No pun intended.

An hour later, we got our bio tests back. Written in red at the top was 85%, with a *Nice work, Darren!* from Mrs. Inrig.

Score!

When I studied, I could get A's. Here was the proof. Maybe if I worked hard I could bring my average up to an A minus by the end of the semester.

My biggest challenge was economics class. Mr. Miller always brought math and stats into it. And he didn't put many notes on the board to study from, so I had to try to summarize everything.

When we all complained, he said he was doing us a favor by preparing us for college.

It didn't help that Miller had hair sprouting from weird places, like the back of his neck and the top of his nose. It distracted me from what he was saying. Somebody oughta slip him a hair trimmer.

Today's lesson was: *How can I be a savvy investor?* Maybe it would be less boring than usual, because this was info I could actually use. One day I planned to have lots of money—legit money.

"Picture you have one hundred thousand dollars," Miller said. "Can you do that?"

We all nodded, and a few people went, "Yeaaah."

"Now, how are you going to invest it? Any ideas?"

"I'd put it all into green energy," Jessica said. She sat at the front of the class on the left side. Since I was at the back right, I could watch her all class long without her knowing it.

"That's a thought," Miller said. "You used the word, 'all.' Do you intend to put all your money in the same place?"

She thought about it. "I'd put all of it into green energy, but maybe in different companies."

"Why?"

Her reply was quick. "Because if one company goes bankrupt, I'd only lose what I'd invested in that company."

"What if the whole sector plummets? Then you've lost everything," Miller pointed out.

Someone at the back of the class said, "What goes up must come down."

I thought about Diamond Tony. *What goes up must come down.* Made sense to me.

"So the key is to di-ver-si-fy," Miller said slowly, and actually wrote it on the board. "Put your money in different areas of the economy. Let's say you've put your money in five different sectors and all your stocks are doing well. What next?"

"Sell your stocks before the market goes down," Adam answered from the second row. "I wouldn't wait for things to go wrong."

"No way, I'd let them ride," Fatima said from the seat behind him.

"Well, that is the question, isn't it? That's the thing about investing, my friends. Studies show that those wanting a quick buck don't do as well as long-term investors. However, if your goal is to buy and hold, it takes nerves of steel. Your hundred thousand could be worth a quarter of a million or more—but *only* if you sell. And likely you won't want to sell if your stocks are doing well. So what do you do?"

"I'd watch the market and when something starts to go wrong, I'd cash out right away," Kelvin said.

"That's what most people would do," Miller said. "The moment something scary happens—a popular stock dips, for example—

people pull out. Of course, when everyone does that, it becomes a self-fulfilling prophecy."

"So what are you saying we should do?" Jessica frowned. "Leave the money in or take it out?"

Man, Jessica was cute even when she was confused. I could tell she was taking the discussion seriously. I bet she planned to have a lot of money one day. That was another thing we had in common.

"When to sell is the biggest question of all," Miller said. "There is no right answer. If there were, no one would lose any money in the stock market."

No right answer. I rolled my eyes. What kind of mark would I get on a test if I wrote that?

He put up his index finger. "There is something to consider, however. It's called a stop-loss policy. You make a deal with yourself that once a stock has gone down a certain amount, say ten percent, you'll sell."

"But stocks drop all the time, then go back up," Fatima said. "Why sell if you think it might go back up?"

Miller spread his hands. "It's all about risk. When a stock starts going down, the only way to guarantee you won't lose more money is to sell."

"I wouldn't sell my stock—I'd probably buy more," Adam said. "Aren't you supposed to buy low?"

"Yes. You are."

I made some more notes. This stuff was going to show up on a test, I could smell it.

"Darren, could you summarize the discussion for us?" Miller asked, making me raise my head from the paper.

"Um . . ."

"Tell us what you've written. You've been making notes, right?"

All heads turned my way. Miller obviously thought I was doing something else, like writing rap lyrics, which he'd caught me doing a few times before. I glanced down at my notes and cleared my throat. No way I was going to look stupid in front of Jessica. "Investing rules. One—don't put all your eggs in one basket. Two—don't count your chickens before they've hatched. And three—know when to cut and run."

To my surprise, Miller smiled. "Excellent summary, Darren. I couldn't have said it better myself."

HOMELAND

Over the next week, I did some creeping around the Cash Stop and snapped a few shots with my phone. Since Biggie worked across the street at Artie's Pizza, there was nothing suspicious about me dropping in for a slice of Meatlover's.

It didn't take a genius to see there was strange stuff going on. Random people came and went from the back of the store at weird times of day and night. I spotted executives there only once, while I was eating pizza on a stool in front of the window. Marcus and two of Diamond Tony's security guys went in through a back door and drove off in an Escalade several minutes later.

None of it was hard intel, but it was enough to pass on to

Prescott. He sounded excited by the tip, and told me it could be the missing puzzle piece he'd been looking for. I felt good about that.

So good I even offered to help Mom with Sunday dinner. She rarely cooked unless there was someone to impress—today Tasha's new boyfriend, George, was coming over. The menu was chicken thighs, Stove Top stuffing, yams, garlic mash, and all that good stuff. Mom made me peel a three-pound bag of apples for apple crisp. I didn't mind, especially because it was my favorite dessert, and Kiki's, too.

Mom cooked in her Sunday sweats, but her hair and makeup were done already in case our guest came early. Nothing upset Mom more than to be caught without her "face" on. What amazed me was that she could prepare vegetables without ruining her crazy-long pink nails.

"So how's school going?" Mom asked, rolling up her sleeves and mashing some potatoes.

The question startled me. She wasn't the type to ask questions. She let me do my thing.

"Fine. Aced my last test."

"That's my baby boy." She beamed with pride.

If I were lying, she wouldn't know it. She certainly hadn't in the past. Mom never asked to see my report cards or talked to my teachers. She was one of ten children, all raised by my nana. From what I'd heard, Nana let her kids do what they wanted—they just had to be home at mealtimes if they wanted to be fed. Mom didn't even live up to that.

When I was finished peeling the apples, I plunked down on the couch. Tasha was watching some Hollywood news show and eyed me suspiciously. She knew what I was going to say.

"We're not watching a game, *baby boy*," she said, pointing at me with the remote. "No. Way."

"But it's the Colts against the Packers. C'mon, Tash. The game's half over by now."

"I don't care if it's got ten seconds left. It's boring. The same teams play each other over and over. What's the point?"

"It's about strategy. You could have the most skilled players in the world, but if they don't know how to psych out the other team, how to anticipate their next move, they're done."

She wasn't listening.

"Your show is mind-numbing crap," I said. That got her attention. "I think Kiki should settle this." Kiki was buzzing around the room with his toy cars, swerving them over furniture and crashing them into each other. "Yo, Kiki, what do you think? Should we watch this show, or watch the game?"

"Game!" Kiki's face lit up. "The game!"

Tasha scowled. "Gimme a break. He just likes the word 'game.' I'm not changing it." She turned up the volume. "I want to hear this part."

It was something about Angelina Jolie adopting another kid. Who cares?

"Even in juvie I got to watch a game now and then," I muttered.

I was tempted to go to my room and watch online, but I didn't want to hole up in my room today. So I got down on the floor to play with Kiki.

Tasha's boyfriend, George, arrived at six sharp. He was an okay guy. They'd met at U of T, where Tasha was studying psychology and he studied math. Mom seemed to think anyone who majored in math had to be brilliant. George would probably end up a teacher, but Mom acted like Tasha had landed a CEO.

Maybe Mom should find herself a George instead of wasting time with losers. Then again, maybe she couldn't land one. She was always complaining about the "slim pickings" out there. Kiki's father had seemed promising for a while, until Mom found out he had another girlfriend. Forget about tracking him down for child support. Last we'd heard, he'd moved back to the Caribbean.

Dinner was good. I made sure to load my plate up high, a habit from juvie, where you didn't get to go back for seconds. Just the thought of juvie made me tense. I shrugged it off and focused on Kiki, who always put a smile on my face. He had this habit of secretly stashing food he didn't like under him, which was why the butt of his pants was always covered in squashed food. I spotted him hiding some bits of chicken and gave him a wink.

I looked around the table at my family and suddenly thought of Jessica. For a second, I pictured what it would be like if she were here having dinner with us.

It could still happen, Jessica and me. But first I had to finish what I started. If Prescott's raid of the Cash Stop went as planned, my work would be done. I could gradually pull away from the game and focus on what I really wanted in my life—music, school, Jessica.

Then I would really be free.

JUVIE

Juvie was full of guys like me, young street dealers taking the fall for bigger players. All we'd wanted was a few extra bucks and some status in neighborhoods where the kingpins were royalty. Stupid, yeah, and we paid the price. The justice system was all about teaching us a lesson. Problem was, the real criminals were sitting in VIP booths drinking Cristal while their minions were doing time.

But it wasn't only guys like me in juvie. There were guys who'd killed and raped, then bragged about it so you'd be scared of them. I had to walk beside them, eat lunch with them, clean floors with them, and sometimes bunk in the same room with them.

In juvie, you needed a survival strategy. You had to choose a role and play it well: bully, follower, comic, psychotic loner, whatever. Mine was the independent who flew under the radar and didn't take sides. But there was one thing I couldn't do: look the other way when it wasn't a fair fight. Maybe I got that from my dad, who became a peacekeeper to help people in war-torn countries. When I saw some pipsqueak getting jumped, I got involved. But do that a few times and you might as well paint a bull's-eye on your back.

The worst of the psychos was Jongo. The second he walked into juvie, he called himself the Original Gangsta, started his own gang, and squashed anyone he didn't like. He went after a friend of mine, White Chris, beating him so bad Chris went blind in one eye, all because he talked back.

I knew that Jongo's reign had to end and that it would end with me. So I started to mess with Jongo's head. I spread rumors about him. Tipped off some guards to interfere with his dealing. Made sure he knew I was behind all of it too. Jongo went to the trouble of smuggling in a razor blade just for me. When he pulled it on me in the TV room, I was ready for him. I knew I had to let him cut me if my plan was going to work, but I sure as hell didn't want to die. He went for my neck, and I dodged him so he only caught my shoulder. I ended up with ten stitches. Jongo ended up in an adult prison.

While I was in juvie, I also learned more about Diamond Tony. I'd only known him as a feared and revered kingpin, but the details I heard from prisoners and guards were ugly. Murders, beatings, intimidation. Lots of kids had gotten locked up or killed because they worked for Tony. I was one of them. And it would continue unless someone stopped him.

I wanted that someone to be me.

THE BUST

At 7:37 Monday morning, my secret cell rang.

"It's Prescott," he said, as if he wasn't the only one with this phone number.

"How'd it go last night?" I'd wanted to lurk in an alley as the cops swarmed the store, but I knew better than to take an unnecessary risk.

"It's not what we thought," Prescott replied. "Tony Walker isn't laundering money through the Cash Stop."

My gut sank. "I'm sorry. I really thought—"

"No apologies necessary, kid. What we got is even better." I could tell he had a wise-ass smirk on his face. "See, Walker's executives *were* making cash drops there. You know why? They were paying the Demon's Sons, who supply the coke for the Diamond Dust."

"Holy. Shit." I swallowed this information whole.

"We've been trying to put a case together against the Demon's Sons for years. They weren't expecting this move, Darren. We've got hard evidence on them now."

"You're saying some of them will be charged?"

"It's not that simple. We can put away a couple of the underlings, like the guy who actually runs the place, but the high rollers are based in California and sure as hell won't be coming back this way anytime soon."

My fist curled in frustration. "So you can't connect Tony."

"Not yet, no. There's no paper trail. He made sure of that."

"Oh." I felt like a fool. Somehow I'd been hoping it would be one tip, one bust, and the cops would find everything they needed.

"Don't let it get you down, Darren. Think about it. We've really hit Walker where it hurts."

That's when it clicked. "Wait a minute. If the Demon's Sons are too spooked to come back here, that means . . ."

"You got it. Our friendly neighborhood drug trafficker is out of a supplier. And trust me, finding new suppliers who can deliver quality product on such a large scale is next to impossible these days."

I couldn't believe it. The Diamond Dust was going to run out! It wasn't what I'd intended to happen—none of this meant Diamond Tony was going to jail. But cutting off his supply was a victory. He'd lose thousands of dollars each day. What would Tony do then?

He was going to be fucking livid.

I felt a rush of satisfaction. *Diamond Tony, you have no idea who you messed with.*

"My boss is happy, Darren," Prescott said. "And you know what that means."

"You're getting a promo?"

"Looks like it." He chuckled. "I'll keep you informed."

Anatomy of a Snitch

In my hood, being a snitch
Is the worst thing you can be
Get the cash for the tip
Take the sting from poverty
Peeps snitching left and right
It's more common than you know
Let your conscience be your guide
The rest is gonna flow
You're behind enemy lines
And you've entered into war
It's not about the money
Time to even up the score.

THE DILUTION

Something's off," Cam said Friday night. "Everybody's complaining about the Dust." It was December, and my toes burned in my sneakers from the cold. Thick snowflakes took their time coming down, covering the ground like a soft carpet. Maybe there'd be enough to make snow angels with Kiki tomorrow.

"Guess it's a weak batch." For days now, I'd suspected that Diamond Tony was diluting the supply to make it last longer, probably with baking soda or some other filler. Even the color was different, more off-white than pure white.

Cam frowned. "That's the thing about Diamond Dust. It's never weak. It's the real deal."

I shrugged. "Maybe one of the guys who mixes skimmed some for himself."

"Yeah, if he wants a bullet in his head."

His words caught me off guard. I'd thought Tony's dealers were too starstruck to see him for who he was: a cold-blooded killer. But obviously Cam knew who he was working for.

"You ever tried some?" I asked.

"Once, a couple years ago."

"And was it as good as they say?"

"Better. You ever been on the Vortex roller coaster at Wonderland?"

"Yeah."

"Picture that times a thousand. The Dust literally blows your mind to pieces." Cam shivered, probably not from cold. "Scared the fuck out of me."

I heard shoes crunching in the snow and turned around to see a fiend approaching me. Torn-up clothes hung off his skinny limbs. He handed me a ten-dollar bill.

"The cost is twenty," I said.

"That's all you getting from me!"

"Sorry, man. I'm not allowed to change the price."

He scoffed. "You're lucky I was too tired to go to them other dealers on the South Side, but I guess I'll have to. Gimme my money."

I gave it back to him and the man stalked off, muttering to himself.

Cam and I looked at each other. The regular users couldn't be fooled. Every day we were losing more customers to the Bloods.

Vinny showed up a few minutes later. He walked with his usual swagger, but his face was serious.

"Something's wrong with the batch, Vinny, I'm telling you," Cam said as we exchanged the product and cash. "We're losing customers. Have you told Tony?"

Vinny's mouth made a grim line. "DT knows about the problem. He'll take care of it. In the meantime, keep pushing."

"Some of the regulars are trying to cut deals," I said. "If we don't start negotiating, they'll all be buying from the Bloods."

"Shit." Vinny's jaw tightened.

I wasn't sure what kind of answer that was. "So can we cut some deals or not?" I asked.

"If you really have to, do it."

"Man, I hope the next batch is better than this," Cam said, shaking his head.

"'Course it will be." But Vinny wasn't very convincing. He was obviously pissing himself about the situation.

Diamond Tony must be in crisis mode. I bet it killed him to lose business to Andre and the Bloods.

How long before Tony told his street dealers he was running out of supply? He probably wouldn't make it another week before it became plain as day. Cam obviously hadn't figured out that the bust of the Cash Stop was related, but I wouldn't be surprised if some of the other dealers saw the connection. The bust had made the news, giving Prescott another chance to brag to reporters.

Since we were done for the night, Cam and I decided to go somewhere. We both had to take a load off after dealing with unhappy customers all week.

"Should we hit a club?" I asked.

"Yeah. You got ID?"

"Of course." I showed it to him.

He scrutinized it. "Good match. Where'd you get it?"

"Friend of a friend hooked me up."

"Nice. How about Chaos?"

"Sure. I've never been."

"You haven't? You're gonna love it, Dare. The waitresses there are Grade A flesh."

I had to smile. "You sound like a butcher."

"I do, don't I? Maybe Zev's Meat Market is hiring." He touched his bushy red hair. "Think a hairnet could tame this?"

I laughed, imagining Cam in an apron and hairnet. It also got me wondering. "If the product doesn't get better, DT's operation is going to downsize."

"True that. You better start making plans. I'm set either way. I'm gonna take my GED."

"Your mama's idea?"

"Nah, it was mine. Sometimes this whole scene gets tired, you know? I might switch it up one of these days."

I hoped Cam was serious. With a turf war brewing, none of us was safe. If Cam was wise, he'd get out before things got ugly.

That was an option I didn't have.

THE CLUB

The pounding music, the smoke from dry ice machines, and the smell of hot bodies hit me all at once. I'd only been to a couple of clubs since I got my fake ID, and it was still a rush.

Chaos was the type of club you'd see in a music video—big and swanky, with velvet VIP booths raised high like thrones. Everybody was dressed up, putting on a show with their expensive clothes and bling. Truth was, most of the people here probably lived in the nearby projects. Pretending to be rich was part of the draw.

Cam and I snagged a table and stuffed our jackets onto the seat. Forget paying the extra five bucks for the coat check. A waitress in a little black dress appeared. Cam started sweet-talking her, and she pretended to be flattered, but I doubted she could even hear him over the thumping noise. It was all part of the game to get our money.

"*Dayum,*" Cam said as she walked off. "That's all I have to say."

Cam surveyed the girls on the dance floor and gave them ratings out of five stars, like he did with cars. Tuning him out, I scanned the place. Jessica Thomas was crossing the club with a tray of drinks. She worked here?

She looked phenomenal in a little black dress that hugged her curves. Her makeup was runway style, with smoky eyes and bloodred lips. I was sure most of the guys were going crazy over her.

Jessica stopped at a table, expertly propping her tray on the side. The guys were obviously loving the view when she bent to put the drinks in front of them. I felt a rush of anger. Jessica was too classy for that.

She checked in with another couple of tables, then went to the bar. I was tempted to go up to her, but what would be the point? I hadn't called her all week, and she'd been avoiding eye contact at school. She thought I'd rejected her, and I couldn't explain why I'd done it.

Our waitress returned with our drinks a few minutes later. Cam tried to convince me to dance so we could meet some girls, but I wasn't up for it, so he went alone. The guy had balls, I'd give him that. Cam started grinding with a girl who didn't even see him behind her. Of course, when her friends pointed out what he was doing, she shoved him away. He struck out a couple more times before he finally gave up.

"The girls here are cold." Cam shuddered. "Next time we go to the Velvet Room." Then something caught his attention. "Hey, look who's rolling in."

I glanced toward the doors. It was Diamond Tony and his entourage. They passed through the club in a cool wave of bling and took up two booths in the VIP section.

Jessica approached them to take their order. I hated the thought of Diamond Tony anywhere near her. Thankfully, he seemed to be plenty occupied with the girls on either side of him.

But that wasn't the case for Marcus, Tony's right-hand man. His eyes were all over Jessica. He cozied up to her, and at one point, he slipped his arm around her waist. She didn't shy away. She just smiled sweetly. If she was uncomfortable, she hid it well. I knew a lot of girls thought Marcus was good-looking, but he was part of the terror monarchy and I hoped Jessica knew enough to stay away.

"I'll be right back," I told Cam.

I followed Jessica to the bar. Before I could tap her shoulder, she turned and bumped into my chest. "Darren."

"Were you hoping I'd show up?" I asked, echoing her words

from last week. I knew that Marcus was watching us.

She didn't seem to know how to answer, so I went on. "You don't want to let Marcus get close to you. He's dangerous."

Her face sobered. "I know. But our manager said to be nice to them, so I'm trying to play along."

"I have an idea to get him off your back. Do you trust me, Jessica?"

She nodded.

Then I kissed her. At first her whole body stiffened, but then she relaxed against me. She opened her lips, and our kiss deepened. She felt amazing. So amazing I didn't want to stop. She moaned against my mouth, and it drove me crazy.

Finally, I felt her hand touch my chest to push me away, but instead she held on to me. "Did he see us?" she asked in my ear.

"I think so. Stop by my table later to reinforce that we're together."

"Okay." She mustered up a smile and went back to work.

I returned to my table. Cam was gaping at me. "Who the hell is that?"

"A girl from school."

"You never said you had a girlfriend."

"It's complicated."

"Looked pretty straightforward to me. Has she got a friend?"

"I'll ask her." I watched Jessica serve drinks to Marcus's table. Relief flooded through me; he'd already cozied up to another girl. I knew that my plan could've backfired—Marcus could've gone after Jessica even if she had a boyfriend. But Marcus had so many women to pick from that he didn't need to bother.

Jessica came to our table with more drinks. I tried to hand her some money, but she said, "On the house," and kissed me right on the lips.

Before she walked away, she said, "I'll call *you*."

AT WAR

Did you hear what happened last night?" Albert asked me eagerly. We were the first to arrive at the meeting late the next morning. Vinny's basement didn't look or smell any better than it had last time.

"No."

"One of Andre's top lieutenants got taken out."

"Nice." If Diamond Tony wanted to start a war with the Bloods, killing a lieutenant was a great way to do it.

"They say he walked up to a car to make a deal, but got a bullet in the chest instead."

"Too bad, so sad." I grinned. "Andre should never have messed with Tony."

"You said it."

Tony's message to Andre was clear: Stealing his customers was unacceptable. Even if his product was crap. Even if he was selling nothing but straight baking soda and calling it Diamond Dust. They were his customers and no one else's.

Within ten minutes, everyone else had arrived. They were hyped up about the murder, praising Tony like he was some kind of hero. But I noticed Cam was quiet. He knew what this meant. The bloodshed had just begun.

Vinny clapped twice to shut us up, then started the meeting. "I want to congratulate y'all on holding shit together during this rough time. You made me proud. DT, too."

"'Course we holding shit down," Albert said. "That's what soljahs do."

Vinny nodded. "I know the fiends have been wilding out, but don't worry. That's gonna change. We've got premium shit that should last us a few weeks until our supply problem is fixed. DT shelled out some serious cash so we can keep the customers satisfied."

I could tell that the other dealers were relieved to hear this. But Vinny said himself that the fix was only temporary. Prescott must've been right about how hard it was to secure new suppliers. I bet Tony had paid several drug dealers shitloads of cash to buy their product. It was a wise move. He was in danger of losing his business if things kept going this way.

"You're going to keep giving out little extras—dope, weed," Vinny went on. "And we're keeping our prices low. The South Side Bloods are greedy as hell, and it's gonna come back to bite them."

"I bet Andre went apeshit after what Tony did to his lieutenant," T-Bone said. "That was slick, yo."

Vinny held up a hand. "The Bloods *will* be coming after us. It'll be today or tomorrow or next month. But it will happen. We've got to be ready. They have no idea about the shit that'll rain down on them if they come after Diamond Tony's people."

"Amen," Albert and Pie said at the same time.

The meeting was over. There was nothing more to say.

Cam and I were the last to step outside. The sun had come out, and I squinted, adjusting to the light against the snow.

I turned to Cam. "Want to get a sub?"

Then I heard a burst of loud pops, like fireworks.

Bullets sprayed the air. Snow dusted up around us in a white cloud.

Down! Go down!

I dropped to the ground, then crawled behind a tree. I peered around it. The bullets were coming from a car parked a few yards from the house. A tinted window in the backseat was lowered and the barrel of a gun stuck out.

If someone got out of the car, I was a sitting duck. I'd have to run, but in which direction?

Behind the house. That's where Cam was headed. Behind the house and over the fence.

The car's wheels spun in the snow, then it sped down the street and took a corner.

I jumped to my feet. A short distance in front of me, two guys were lying on the ground. I ran up to one of them and grabbed the back of his jacket. Pie struggled, like he thought I was attacking him.

"Easy, easy. It's Darren. You hit?"

"I don't know!" He frantically felt over his body, which told me he wasn't hit.

I went to Albert. When I turned him onto his side, I saw the blood. So much blood. Albert's eyes stared into mine. I could see he was scared and struggling to breathe. Most of the bleeding was coming from his abdomen. Taking off my coat, I applied pressure like I'd seen on TV.

"Goddamn . . . ," Albert muttered, then his eyes lost focus.

People surrounded us. In the distance, sirens blared.

I moved away when the paramedics came. They tried to revive

him. For several minutes everybody stood around watching as they worked on him.

It was too late. Albert was gone.

I kept thinking of what Vinny had said.

It'll be today or tomorrow or next month. But it will happen.

BLIND

What if I'd been the first to walk outside? I kept asking myself. What would have gone through my mind while I was bleeding out in the snow?

I wondered if Albert's life had flashed before his eyes and whether he'd seen a white light. I wondered if he'd been in pain, or if, at the moment of death, he'd felt numb.

I didn't want to think about it. But I couldn't focus on anything else.

Around midnight I got a text from Jessica.

Meet me after work?

I texted back: *Ok.*

It was too late to pretend I wasn't into her. The kiss at the club had given me away. And the truth was, I didn't want to be alone. I needed some Jessica right now.

At 2:05, Jessica left the club in a faux-fur coat and leather boots. She saw me on the sidewalk and gave me a hug that warmed me through our coats.

"There's a place around the corner," she said, hooking her arm through mine. I didn't know if she was worried about slipping on the ice or if she wanted to be close to me, but I liked it either way.

Jessica took me to a Middle-Eastern diner. Huge hunks of chicken and beef rotated on spits behind the counter, filling the air with the mouthwatering smells of spicy meat. The place was empty except for a group of old Arab guys sitting at the counter, chatting with the owner. We ordered hot chocolates and sat down.

"I heard what happened today," she said. "Are you okay?"

I hesitated. Was this why she'd wanted to meet with me—to get the gory details? But no, that wasn't Jessica.

"I'm fine."

"Must've been scary. Anyone could've gotten hit."

"I know."

She obviously expected me to say something more, something deep, but I didn't know what that was.

"I'm surprised you got back into the game after juvie," she said after a moment.

There it was. The question nobody had dared to ask. Jessica was even bolder than I'd thought. She must've been nervous, though—her napkin was torn to pieces in front of her.

I played it cool. "Nobody wants to hire you out of juvie. Anyway, this is a temporary thing."

"My boss is looking for another coat check person. I could ask him for you."

"Thanks, but don't worry about it."

Jessica didn't want me selling drugs. That made me respect her even more. But I wondered why she'd bothered with me in the first place.

I changed the topic. "So how'd you end up working at Chaos?"

"My friend Natalie works there, so she got me an interview."

I raised an eyebrow teasingly. "How does an interview work? You put on a tight skirt and heels and walk with a tray?"

"Ha-ha. The tips are amazing. I had to work at Wendy's five nights a week to make the same money I make Friday and Saturday nights. And if I wasn't already working there, I'd be trying to find a way in."

"I don't blame you. I'm just worried you'll slip on all those guys' drool."

"Very funny," she said, fighting a smile.

Warmth spread through my chest, and it wasn't the hot drink. Jessica was achingly sweet. The memory of our kiss filled my mind. I zoned out for a few seconds, reliving every hot moment, then started listening to her again. She was saying how much she loved my music.

"I'm going to make it my career," I told her. "Me and a friend are planning to start up a record label."

"That's exciting. I wish I could be involved somehow."

"Do you sing?"

"Very badly."

"You can dance in one of our videos, then. I know you can dance."

She fluttered her lashes downward, and I bet she was thinking back to Smalls's party, where we'd gotten so close there wasn't a breath of space between us. I wished we could be that close right now.

"If you liked my dancing so much, you should've called me."

Did she have to put me on the spot like that? She knew I was interested. I wouldn't be here at two thirty in the morning if I wasn't.

"I've been focused on the streets. Lot of shit going down."

Her eyes went big. "Oh." She was thinking about Albert's murder, of course. She must've heard about Rico's murder too. "I'm sorry. I didn't realize that's why you didn't call." She looked worried. About me.

"Don't be sorry. You hungry? I'm thinking about a chicken shawarma."

"I'll have one too."

I went up to the counter to get the food. When I came back, I made sure we stayed on safe topics. School. Filimino's grading methods. Gossip—that was Jessica's territory. But instead of trash-talking people, she managed to make excuses for them, no matter what they were into. The girl didn't have a mean bone in her body. I guess I should be glad; if she were more judgmental, she wouldn't be hanging with me.

By the time she suggested we leave, the sky was lightening. I wasn't even tired. Being with Jessica made my blood buzz. We headed outside and hailed a cab.

In the backseat, the tension between us was electric. We sat right against each other, and she laid her head on my shoulder. When she looked up at me, I couldn't resist kissing her. She cupped the back of my head and kissed me back. Her kiss was slow and sensual. There was no staying away from Jessica. No pretending I was indifferent. I wanted her more than I'd wanted any girl.

I knew that I was lost. And it was the best place I'd ever been.

Lost

That girl is a rocket ship
She blasts you up so high

TAKEDOWN

That girl is a lightning bolt
Flash of brilliance in the sky
For that girl you'd do anything
Everything
Anything
For that girl you'd do anything
Even give your life.

WHITE CHRIS

Be careful out there, Darren. This isn't over. Walker will hit back. One of his dealers is dead, and he has to save face."

Prescott's words echoed in my brain as I rode the subway to meet up with White Chris. Weird, but when I'd called Prescott that morning, I'd half expected him to tell me to get out of the game. To say that it was too dangerous.

Maybe part of me *wanted* to get out. But I was just being weak. If I abandoned my mission, the bodies would keep piling up.

I got to Local's Restaurant before White Chris and ordered a basket of suicide-hot wings. Local's was a dark, seedy place, but I didn't care because the food was good, cheap, and there was lots of it.

The waitresses were old but still showed off their wrinkly goods, and the same men always hung out at the bar hoping some woman would take them home. TVs were all over the place showing different games. Sometimes White Chris and I watched, hardly talking at all. Other times, we made plans for our record label and wrote lyrics.

Today, though, I needed to talk.

White Chris strolled in a few minutes later, his baggy clothes dangling off his lanky six-foot-three frame. The way he dressed, you'd never know his parents had money. But you could tell by the way he talked that he was from the suburbs—that's why the guys in juvie called him White Chris.

"Hey." He sat down, helping himself to a chicken wing.

White Chris was more than a friend, he was a brother. He'd been in juvie for two months when I got there, and he had given me the lowdown on which guards were cool and which never to piss off. That knowledge was key to my survival. I just wished I'd been there when he was cornered by Jongo and his gang. I'd been working in the laundry that morning, clueless about what was happening to my friend. I'd do anything to go back in time to stop the beating that'd left him half-blind. Someone should've had his back, and it should've been me.

White Chris was one of those suburban kids who got into trouble because he was so damned bored. He'd learned how to hot-wire cars from YouTube. He didn't even sell the cars he jacked. He did it for the rush, then dropped them off in random spots.

One day he saw an opportunity he couldn't pass up—a car parked in front of an ice cream shop. The driver hadn't bothered to lock her doors before she went inside. Chris hopped in and drove off. He'd only made it down the street when a toddler said from the backseat, "Ice cweam?" That part of the story always cracked me up.

So Chris pulled over right away. Nice guy that he was, he put down the windows so the kid could have some air and even called in an anonymous tip to tell the police where the kid was. Too bad there was a cop car one block away. Chris got caught, and the press had a field day with the whole thing: privileged suburban kid joyrides with toddler in the backseat. Chris got locked up for eighteen months.

I told him about Albert. When I finished talking, I felt drained, but lighter. Chris stared at me with his good eye. I'd learned to focus on that eye, not the one that had a swirl of yellow where the pupil should be.

"Maybe you should rethink your plan," he said.

"What plan?"

He snorted. "Come on. You cursed Diamond Tony out the whole time you were in juvie. Now you expect me to believe you just up and went to work for him again? I know you."

Holy shit. He might be half-blind, but he saw right through me.

"Why didn't you say anything?" I asked.

"No point. I wasn't going to try to talk you out of it. But now I am. It's not worth getting yourself killed over this revenge thing."

"It's not only about me. It's for everybody."

"Like with Jongo, huh? You were going to get him out of there no matter what you had to do. That was some crazy shit you pulled. You could've gotten yourself killed."

"But you're not sorry I did it," I pointed out.

"Hell, no! Jongo got what was coming to him." His face darkened. "But if you'd been killed, then I'd be sorry. That's the thing, Darren. You don't know how this is gonna turn out."

"You don't have to worry. I'm watching my back."

"I'm sure you are. There's just one thing you've got to realize."

"Oh yeah?" I wasn't sure I wanted to know.

"You're not smarter than Diamond Tony."

"I'm not saying I am."

"You think you're gonna outsmart him, but you won't. Look, I'm on your side. I want you to squash that motherfucker. I'm just not sure you can do it."

I didn't say anything. Of all people, I could count on White Chris to tell me the truth. Unlike Prescott, he wasn't looking for a promotion.

"If I try to get out now, they might think I was the snitch who told the Bloods the location of our meeting—not that I'm thinking of getting out."

"Do what you want. But I need you around to drive when we take girls out. I can't be taking them on the subway all the time."

"You know I don't have a car."

"Want me to jack one for you?" He smiled. "At least you've got your license. That's more than I'll ever have."

"I hear you. I'll get us a car when this is all over," I promised.

"Let's hope you'll be alive to drive it."

There it was again, the darkness in his expression. I didn't like being confronted with his fears, because they were mine, too.

It was cool hanging out with White Chris, but sometimes he saw too much.

HOLIDAY DEALS

His name is Darren/You'll never hear him swearin'/Because he's really carin'." Jessica and I were in her bedroom. She rapped while I did some beat-boxing. Her goal was always to make the worst lyrics possible.

"Wait, I've got something better." She cleared her throat. "Darren has nice cologne/But don't leave him home alone/He'll be eating a calzone."

I cracked up, and so did she. The more time I spent with her, the more I realized that Jessica wasn't only beautiful and sexy, she was funny as hell. And she loved to laugh at herself.

The Christmas holidays were under way, and we were spending

all of our free time together. It just happened that way. If one of us needed something at the mall, the other would go along. If there was a movie one of us wanted to see, the other went too. If her mom was cooking something good, she told me to come right over. Truth was, everything was better with Jessica by my side.

Jessica lived in a three-bedroom apartment with her parents and thirteen-year-old sister, Kendra. As families went, hers was solid. She had two parents who seemed to like each other. Parents who actually gave a shit and asked the right questions. They weren't happy about Jessica waitressing at the club, but they said it was her choice. As for me, they'd welcomed me warmly. But I knew that wouldn't last if they found out I was a dealer.

Jessica's bedroom was twice the size of mine and as picture perfect as she was. The walls were pastel pink with a thick yellow stripe around the middle—Jessica said she'd done the painting herself. All of the furniture was white IKEA, draped with silky fabric or done up with colorful designs. She had a dozen nail polishes on her dresser, arranged by color, and a neatly organized bookshelf. Nothing was out of place, except for the pile of socks that were peeking out from under her bed.

"I'm starting to think you're not going to want me to write lyrics for your album." Jessica bit her lip against a laugh.

"Your lyrics are definitely . . . unique." I smirked. "It's a shame I already have a writing partner."

"Oh yeah. What was his name again?"

"White Chris."

"*White* Chris?"

"A nickname from juvie. He lives in a big house in the burbs. His dad's a principal and his mom's an English prof."

"Hope I'll meet him sometime." She paused. Jessica never ran out of things to say, so I knew something was up. "Are you afraid of going to juvie again?"

"If I was, would I still be dealing?"

"I'm not sure. Maybe it's the only way you can keep status."

"You sound like a shrink." I stretched out on her bed like it was my own, folding my hands behind my head. "So where are you taking me today? I hope I don't have to smell more perfumes."

"I wouldn't do that to you two days in a row. Today you can watch me try on jeans."

"So I'm gonna have to say you don't look fat in a million different ways."

She giggled. "Get practicing, honey."

I looked her up and down. "You look good in those jeans, Jessica. So good you don't even need to wear pants at all."

"Darren!" She dove on top of me. I caught her arms, rolled her under me, and kissed her.

Kissing Jessica was my favorite thing to do these days. All

thought and worry left my brain, and there was nothing but the feel of her against me.

"I've wanted you for so long, Darren," she whispered against my lips.

"Oh yeah?"

"I had a serious crush on you in junior high. But you never paid any attention to me, or any girl, really."

"Are you kidding? If I'd known, I'd have been all over you."

"You're all over me now."

"Not the way I'd like to be."

She whispered in my ear, "Not yet, Darren."

The tickle of her breath in my ear only made my heart pump harder. "Whatever you want. You're the boss. I'm the humble employee ready to do anything you like." I kissed the sweet spot behind her ear. "Anything at all."

An hour later we were at the mall. So was everyone else in the neighborhood. It was the place to be seen, to show off your threads, hair, bling. And now everyone was scrambling for last-minute Christmas gifts. Not Jessica, though. She'd finished a month ago.

"Let's go into Dynamite. I need that jacket." It wasn't Jessica talking, it was her sister. Kendra looked like a mini Jessica, except she had pink braces and a different nose. That was the catch of spending so much time with Jessica—sometimes Kendra tagged along. It was annoying, but part of the deal.

My cell buzzed. It was a text from Vinny. A reminder of the streets I didn't need.

"You still haven't gotten a gift for Mom yet," Jessica was saying to Kendra.

"I know. I'll only be a minute," she insisted.

"I'm gonna sit this one out." I parked myself on a bench outside the store.

"We won't be long," Jessica said.

"No worries." I was already reading the text.

Hey d. Good news. Found new rims. Watching empire strikes back w the boys. Merry xmas hahaha.

Yeah, it was real good news. I wondered what chumps Vinny had found to replace Albert and Pie. The job description wasn't very appealing: Take over from a guy who got shot to death and his best friend who was so wired with post-traumatic stress that he had to be taken off the streets. I bet Vinny found a couple of lookouts who wanted to move up in the ranks, kids as dumb as I used to be. Kids who saw the turf war as nothing but a video game.

The Empire Strikes Back—Vinny's way of saying that Tony was plotting payback. That was a no-brainer. Everyone knew it was only a matter of time.

When the girls came back, I was wearing my it's-all-good face. "How'd it go?" I asked.

"Great!" Kendra swung her shopping bag. "Did you see me try it on?"

I shook my head.

"I'll show you! Hold this." She gave Jessica her other purchases, then took out the jacket—dark blue denim with purple embroidered flowers—and started posing. "Well?"

"It's nice." Girls liked compliments, even meaningless ones.

Kendra clapped her hands with excitement.

"It would've been cheaper after Christmas," Jessica said.

"Yeah, but there were only two left in my size!"

"Kendra's right," I said. "You can't pass up a jacket like that. Fashion first."

Jessica laughed, punching my arm. I squeezed her to my side and whispered in her ear, "I love it when you manhandle me. Do that again."

"You wish." I saw a flash of heat in her eyes, then she wriggled away. "Let's go to the toy store. I know you already have a gift for Kiki, but there's something I want you to see."

Curious, I followed her.

The toy store was packed, of course. Moms and dads were racing through the aisles with shopping carts filled sky-high. Good thing Jessica knew exactly where she was going.

"Here it is."

It was a box of toddler-sized musical instruments: an electric guitar, a drum, a tambourine, and a pair of shakers. "You could add this, too." She picked up a small keyboard. "It's got all these different settings. Kiki could make rhymes like you. I was reading this book that said if you want to be great at something, truly great, you have to start young. If Kiki starts making music now, think of how amazing he'll be by the time he's our age."

I couldn't believe she'd put so much thought into a gift for Kiki. "Thanks, Jessica." But *thanks* didn't cover how impressed I was with this girl. "This is perfect. I'm gonna get it. I'll save the trucks for his birthday."

As we got in line for the checkout, I was pumped. I'd never been so excited to give a gift. All I ever got Mom and Tasha were gift cards for the beauty shop. Jessica was right—I could teach Kiki so much about music. He could be my protégé.

After I bought the instruments, we headed for the food court and got something to eat. I sat back and watched the crowd while Jessica and Kendra talked about some actress I'd never heard of.

"She's totally fugly," Kendra said between licks of frozen yogurt.

"No way. She's unique. Not everyone has to be stick thin with fake boobs, you know." Jessica turned to me for backup. "What do you think?"

"I think you should have some poutine." I dangled a gooey forkful of fries and cheese in front of her. "Come on."

She went for it. "Mmm."

"My man Darren!" a voice said from behind me.

I didn't have to turn around to know who it was.

Shit.

"Hey, Vinny."

Vinny was pimped out in fur and blinged in ice, a ghetto version of Kanye West. His tray was piled high with burgers and fries, and some shopping bags were slung over his arm. Two guys stood with him. One of them wore glasses and impeccable clothes; the other had a shaved head and tattoos crawling up his neck. I was pretty sure they were lieutenants, but I didn't know their names. All I knew was that I didn't want them anywhere near Jessica and Kendra.

"You got my text?" Vinny asked me.

I gave a quick nod. He'd better not say more about it.

Vinny and the lieutenants snagged the table next to us. Before Vinny could open his trap again, I said, "How about the game?"

I prayed Vinny would take the bait. He was a die-hard Raptors fan, and last night's loss would be his latest heartbreak.

"Shadiest game ever!" Vinny thumped a fist on the table. "We almost had it. Somebody's paying off the refs, I swear."

The tattooed lieutenant scoffed. "You ain't serious. The Knicks could wipe the court with them any day of the week."

As the debate took off, I glanced at Jessica and Kendra, who were still eating their frozen yogurt. If the lieutenants' talk switched away from basketball, they could easily mention the biz. The last thing I wanted was for Kendra to know I was a dealer. She was young enough and keen enough to march right up to Jessica's parents with what she knew. Then I'd be screwed.

I tapped my foot under the table. "Let's go get that gift for your mom," I said to Kendra.

She shrugged, savoring her frozen yogurt. That girl had to be the slowest eater ever. "I can't bring this into the store with me."

"No one will notice," Jessica said, pushing away her own frozen yogurt. She was probably thinking the same thing I was. "They could sell out if we don't hurry."

The conversation at Vinny's table suddenly stopped. One of the lieutenants said, "Bloods, two o'clock."

I scanned the vicinity. There were four of them. And they weren't your regular neighborhood Bloods flashing their colors—they were South Siders who worked the corners for Andre. I'd seen them before.

The Bloods were looking straight at us.

Every muscle in my body tightened. I had no doubt that they were strapped. Vinny and the lieutenants would be too.

I put a hand to my side, as if I was armed. "Damn it, DT wants us to stand down," I said in a low voice, trying to remind them that Tony wouldn't want a shoot-out. I only hoped I was right. Problem was, I didn't know if Tony's orders to stand down applied to his lieutenants or just his street dealers.

Vinny and the lieutenants turned toward the Bloods, their stares issuing a challenge. I had my answer. They weren't avoiding a confrontation, they were inviting it.

The Bloods' stances hardened, and their hands shifted to their sides for easy access.

Out of the corner of my eye, I saw Kendra shrivel in her seat. Even if she hadn't heard me, she felt the tension crackling in the air. Jessica put a protective arm around her.

I had no weapon. No exit strategy. My only plan was to throw my body over Jessica and Kendra to shield them.

Seconds ticked away. The soft roar of the crowd seemed to fade into silence as the shoppers became nothing more than extras in a movie.

It was up to the Bloods. If they didn't keep going, it was on.

One of them muttered something to the others, who nodded grudgingly. They started walking. But their eyes never left our table until they were around the corner.

I could breathe again.

Vinny smirked. "Buncha pussies, walking away like that."

"Bet they wanted to break into a run," the lieutenant with the glasses said, and they all slapped hands.

I didn't see it that way. I could tell those Bloods were as hot-headed as the lieutenants. The fact that they'd walked away meant one thing: They had orders from Andre to stand down.

That was interesting. Andre had only been head of the Bloods for a few months, but he obviously had a tight rein on his soldiers. And he was smart—too smart to let them start something in a crowded mall.

Andre actually had the chops to be a leader. The question was, did he have a chance against Tony?

WRITTEN IN STONE

Christmas morning was snowy. It was a pretty scene, even in Jane-Finch, like one of those snow globes. I spent the morning on the floor with Kiki, who went wild over the music set. I accompanied him on the keyboard while he pounded on the drum and sang words I couldn't figure out. He had natural rhythm.

It was my first Christmas with him, and I ended up singing songs I thought I'd forgotten the words to. Whenever I thought of all the important things I'd missed by being in juvie, it tore me up. Kiki's first smiles, first steps, first words. I wasn't his dad, but I was the closest thing he'd have to one.

Christmas in juvie was the shittiest time of year. The little plastic tree in the cafeteria made us all feel worse. The only good thing was that White Chris and I had been inspired to write a rap called "White Chris-mas," about a guy who broke out of juvie on Christmas Eve, then set the place on fire. It was going to be our first single, and hopefully it would blow up.

Mom made French toast, our Christmas tradition. She used thick Texas toast and sprinkled it with cinnamon and icing sugar. Kiki made a mess of himself, getting food all over his face and hair, but that was part of the fun. When Kiki was done eating, he reached out to me with powdery hands, and even though I knew it would get my shirt dirty, I lifted him out of his booster seat. We went to the sink and washed up, then got down on the floor again to play with his new toys.

That afternoon, Jessica stopped by. When I opened the door, she wrapped her arms around my neck and kissed me. I might've enjoyed it if Mom and Tasha weren't watching. They'd already met Jessica a few times, but I still wasn't comfortable with them all in the same room.

"Jessi!" Kiki ran to her, and she scooped him up. He nuzzled her neck and started playing with her hair like a new toy. He'd been hooked on her instantly, and I couldn't blame him. She looked good, smelled good, and gave lots of hugs.

"Easy, Kiki, you're messing up her hair," I said.

"It's okay," Jessica said. "You'll have to help me brush it, right, Kiki?"

"Brush, brush!" He smoothed her hair.

We all laughed. I loved seeing Jessica with Kiki, seeing how good she treated him.

"Have you eaten, Jessica?" Mom asked. "I made a ton of French toast this morning."

"Thanks, but I'm stuffed." Jessica put a hand over her stomach. "We just had brunch. And I'll be expected to eat again in a few hours."

"You're probably thirsty, then," Mom said, and Jessica agreed to some juice. Mom obviously wanted to impress her. She saw how sophisticated Jessica was, and I could tell she was proud that I was with her. Tasha just looked bored. No one I could bring home would ever impress her, because she'd wonder what they saw in me.

Jessica took a present from her bag. "I have a gift for you."

Kiki's eyes lit up. "Toys!"

She helped him with the shiny red wrapping paper, revealing a package of fifteen Matchbox cars. Kiki squealed and struggled to tear the package open until Mom intervened with scissors.

As Kiki played with his cars, my mom chatted with Jessica. More like, Mom pelted her with questions, some of them too personal.

"So, Jessica, Darren hasn't told me much about your family. What do your parents do?"

I wanted to throw one of Kiki's cars at her. Mom was all about status, and she was way too obvious about it.

"My mom's a personal support worker, and she's going to night school for social work. Dad's the executive chef at Luigi's."

"Wow. *Executive* chef." Mom was really impressed. "You must eat well at your place."

"Well, when he's home, the last thing he wants to do is cook. My mom does most of it. She's pretty good, though."

Mom's questions went on, but Jessica answered cheerfully. It was a relief when Kiki went for his nap and Jessica and I finally got the chance to be alone. In my bedroom, we put on some music.

"Sorry about my mom," I said, lying down on the bed. "She doesn't know when to quit."

Jessica cuddled in to me. "She wants to make sure I'm good enough for her son."

"Nah, she's just trying to figure out why you're bothering with me."

"No way. Your mom adores you. I can tell."

"What about Tasha—she adore me too?"

She paused. "Your sister's more reserved than your mom."

"Nice of you to put it that way. I'd call her cold."

"Now, Kiki, in my opinion, is the cutest kid ever. He has your wicked smile."

"You think I have a wicked smile?"

"Sure. Cute *and* dangerous."

"Oh yeah? You like a dangerous guy?"

"Not really. But you're not a dangerous guy, deep down."

I wasn't sure what to think of that. What I was doing these days was dangerous. "You're not going to tell me I'm a good guy, are you? That's the kiss of death."

She giggled. "You're definitely not good." Her lips touched mine, then softly opened.

We kissed for a while, but Jessica refused to fool around in case Mom came knocking. I told her that my mom wouldn't walk in, but Jessica was too shy about it. She had no clue what she did to me, how much she made me want her. Eventually, Jessica put a hand on my chest and gently pushed me away. She was quiet for a while.

"I was really scared yesterday," she said.

I'd been hoping she wouldn't bring it up. "Yeah. It was weird."

"Weird?" She eased out of my arms. "Is that how you'd put it?"

"Weird. Tense. Look, Jessica, I hated that we were in that situation. I couldn't have predicted it."

"There's no way we're taking Kendra out with us again," she said.

"You're right."

"She knows about you now."

"I figured."

"She thinks I'm a hypocrite for being with a dealer. I've always told her to stay away from—"

"Guys like me," I said wearily. "It's good advice." *So why aren't you taking it?*

"Yeah, well, it's meaningless now. She was going to tell my parents, you know."

"You talked her out of it?"

Jessica nodded. "I said if she did, I'd tell them that I caught her cutting school."

"I'm sorry." And I was. I hated that I'd caused these problems between Jessica and her sister. But I was glad her parents hadn't found out about me. I wanted a future with Jessica when my mission was done.

"I don't see why you have to do it," she said. "I mean, there are people who hate you, who maybe even want to kill you, just because of who you work for."

"Stop, Jessica. You know the deal with me. You've always known it. If you're not comfortable, you're not locked into this."

"I know, but . . ." She sounded defeated. "I know. It just doesn't fit, Darren. You're not one of them. You have so much talent. You don't need them."

"I need *you*." Maybe it sounded dumb, but it was true. With Jessica by my side, I felt like Superman. I could do anything.

Even take down a kingpin.

I kissed her again. She melted in to me, her arguments falling away. Part of me wished she was stronger, that she could get up and walk out of here. It was the smart thing to do. But she couldn't do that. And I couldn't either.

At some point we both fell asleep, because it was after five when I opened my eyes. I sensed Jessica was awake too.

"When do you have to be home for dinner?"

"I have to be at my aunt's at six." She groaned. "I should leave now." But she didn't move from my arms. "I'm dreading it."

"Why?"

"It's our first Christmas without my cousin Valerie."

I'd heard about what happened to Valerie Mays. She was a senior at our school who'd died in a car accident a few months back. She used to hang out with Jessica. I hadn't realized they were related.

"I'm sorry." I didn't know what else to say.

"It's okay. It's just that my family . . . it's like there's this black cloud."

"Must be hard losing someone so close."

She was silent for a moment. "My family says it was her time, that God meant for her to go when she did. They think that if it wasn't a car accident, it would've been something else. But I don't think it was fate. Valerie had so much more to do. So many plans."

"It's easier for people to believe in fate. If you think it's all planned out ahead of time, then you don't have to wonder if you could've changed it."

"What do you think?"

"I don't know." I thought about it. If fate did exist, then for some reason my dad had been assigned a tragic one. I hoped it wouldn't be the same for me. "I'd like to think we make our own."

White Chris-mas

They called him White Chris
Though his skin was so black
Some other inmates
They went on the attack
Time for a prison break
That's how it's got to go
Christmas Eve was the day
Bare feet in the snow
He slips past the guards
Mom's gift around his neck
A pendant of St. Michael
White Chris he will protect

Outside the brick walls
A canister is hid
Put there by a friend
Then a lighter is lit
The flames spread like fear
The flames burn like tears
The walls of juvie burn
The flames of wasted years.
White Chris sits on a hill
Watches the fiery sight
"Merry Chris-mas to all
And to all a good night."

PARANOIA

You're supposed to start a new year optimistic, but I was unsettled as hell.

Now that we were in business again, the customers had flooded back. Night after night, Cam and I stood out there, putting ourselves on the line. I told myself that it was worth the risk, that what I was doing with Prescott meant something. But then I'd see a car drive by slow or a suspicious guy hanging around, and I'd wonder if I should get out while I still could.

"How's your girl?" Cam asked. "Whenever I see you guys, you're all happy and shiny and shit. Makes me wanna throw up."

"She's the Diamond Dust and I'm the addict. I'm hooked, begging for my next hit."

"You lucky dog. I'm still waiting for you to introduce me to her friend, or even her ugly aunt Milly. I'm too horny to be picky."

"I'll see what I can do." I wanted to help the guy out, but Jessica's friends were pretty classy, and I couldn't see any of them going for Cam.

I wished I could be with Jessica instead of freezing on this corner. Now that we were back at school, we had a lot less time together. We'd hung out every day over the holidays, and I was going through withdrawal.

"Re-up time," Cam said.

Vinny got out of his warm and toasty car wearing a long fur coat. He might as well wear a sign saying *Drug Dealer* or *Pimp*. I bet it was made from ferret or some other exotic animal. Maybe someone should sic PETA on his ass.

"Yo, Darren." We pounded knuckles and I gave up the money, subtle like. Not that subtle mattered much when everyone, including the cops, knew what was going on here and on every other corner. "Been a good night, huh?" He slipped the thick wad of cash into his jacket.

"Real good."

"It's calm out? Nothing suspicious?"

I shook my head. "It's cool."

"No cops bugging y'all?"

"Nah."

"Good. Cops are flashing their badges all over the place these days."

"If they think they can touch our man DT, they're stupider than I thought," I said.

Vinny slowly grinned, reminding me of the Joker in *Batman*. "The cops don't think DT's got the balls to hit back. They're wrong. One of them should be wearing a bulletproof vest tonight, know what I'm saying?" Then he went over to Cam to make the exchange and headed back to his car.

I stared after him, reeling. I couldn't believe it. Tony had put a hit out on a cop.

And I knew who that cop was.

Prescott.

It had to be him. He was the public face of the investigation. He was the one who'd gone on TV and threatened to take the kingpin down.

Slow down, I told myself. Maybe Vinny was blowing smoke. Was Tony really loco enough to go after a cop? It would put him at the top of the department's hit list, and that was the last thing he needed. Everybody knew cop killing was out of the question. That shit only went down in Mexico. Besides, Tony's priority was the turf war with the Bloods, wasn't it?

A customer came up behind me looking for a hit, and I almost jumped out of my skin. He handed me the money and I signaled Cam.

We did another couple of deals. The bad feeling in my gut wasn't going away—it burned like an ulcer. Cold sweat broke out all over my body. I had to get in touch with Prescott. Not tomorrow. Not later tonight. *Now.*

Problem was, I wasn't allowed to leave my spot, and I couldn't do it without Cam knowing. If you had to piss, you pissed in the alley. But the cell phone Prescott had given me was tucked under my mattress at home.

I had to risk it.

"Cam," I said, approaching him with a hand on my stomach. "Yo, I ate some bad Chinese."

He made an "ew" look. "You're all sweaty, man."

That was the upside of freaking out. It made for a convincing case of the shits.

"I gotta go home for a minute," I said, half doubled over. "You got this covered?"

"Yeah. Go."

I bolted down the alley and across the lawn, trying to keep to the few trees and shrubs that were growing there. I hoped the shade would disguise my identity. I didn't want anyone to see me running and wondering what I was up to.

I got to my building. Nobody was in the lobby, luckily.

When I hit the apartment, I went straight to my room and locked the door. I dropped to my knees, reached under the mattress for the phone, and pressed #1 for the only number it ever dialed.

The phone rang several times, then Prescott's voice mail picked up. It was Monday night. Was he watching TV with his wife or rocking the twins to sleep? Couldn't he still answer the damn phone?

The voice mail beeped. "Be careful. Tony put a hit out on a cop. I think it's you." I shoved the phone under my mattress, and bolted out of the apartment as my mom hurled questions after me.

When I got back to my corner, I was out of breath.

"Feel better?" Cam asked, hanging back like I was contagious.

"For now, yeah."

All that sweating had made me cold and shaky inside my jacket. I hoped I had it wrong. I hoped I'd taken Vinny too seriously and scared Prescott for nothing.

I didn't want to think of the alternative.

ONE FOR THE PEOPLE

That night I stared at the clock. Prescott didn't call me back on the secret cell. Didn't text. I knew it didn't mean anything. He was probably sleeping, snoring like a freight train or pacing the twins' bedroom, a screaming kid on each arm.

I must've drifted off, because my alarm woke me. I did my morning routine, then grabbed my choco-latte on the way to the bus stop.

"You look like shit," Trey said.

"Thanks." Count on Trey to tell you the truth. I sipped my drink. "So what's our forecast today?"

Trey liked it when I asked about the weather. "Sunny and cold. Risk of flurries tonight."

As Trey dove into the five-day forecast, Biggie and Smalls bounced up to us, giddy about something.

"Crazy shit about that cop!" Smalls said.

I held my breath, like I was at the top of a roller coaster waiting for the plunge. "What cop?"

"You know, the one who's been messing with Tony," Smalls replied. "He's dead. Somebody shot him up outside his house."

"It's all over the news," Trey said, adjusting the strap of his Batman backpack. "His name was Edward Prescott."

I sucked in some cold air, then coughed. I couldn't afford to show what I was feeling. "That's hardcore. Didn't think cops were on Tony's hit list."

"Everybody's saying it's because he went on TV," Smalls said. "The guy kept talking about cleaning up the neighborhood and pushing out the dealers. Pissed off Diamond Tony for sure."

Biggie nodded. "One cop down, one for the people."

They thought Prescott's death was a victory for them, for all of us. I curled my hand into a fist, tempted to smash their faces. But instead I pounded fists with them. "One for the people."

On the way to school, I played along. I had no choice. But my mind was far away. I kept hearing the twins crying, with no daddy to rock them down.

At school, my mind was too messed up to concentrate. I had

this sick feeling that Prescott's death was my fault. If I hadn't helped him get to Pup, he wouldn't have been on TV and on Diamond Tony's radar. Had he even gotten my message?

I felt a stab of panic. Tony would've had guys tailing Prescott. They could have seen me with him. If so, my days were numbered. But I hadn't met with Prescott for weeks—hopefully Tony had made the decision to take him out since then. If Tony knew I was a snitch, he would've had me killed by now.

Unless he'd wanted to take Prescott out first.

I ditched school at lunchtime and walked the streets. I saw deals going down left and right, little baggies and cash slipped from hands into pockets. I saw plainclothed officers sitting in cars. I saw a couple of Diamond Tony's lieutenants scoping the hood, more vigilant than usual.

Tony probably expected a swarm of cops to rain down on his people. Maybe some of Prescott's buddies would bust a few heads. There'd be no point, though. It wouldn't bring him back. It wouldn't give him justice.

Something in the air around me changed. I knew that feeling, and I knew better than to ignore it. I glanced over my shoulder. An old Ford was circling the block and heading back my way. I heard the *vroom* as the driver pressed harder on the gas.

Instinct took over.

Run.

I darted for the projects. The car swerved, then barreled onto the sidewalk and across the lawn—after me. I ran at full blast, but it was right behind me.

Run, run, run! I felt the car driving on my heels, like it could mow me down any second. Two other cars came at me from both sides—cop cruisers. What the hell?

The car behind me suddenly braked, and somebody jumped out. Shouting. I stopped running and put up my hands. Relief flashed through me. *It's just the cops. Not Tony.*

They came at me all at once, knocking me to the ground. I threw out my arms to prevent my head from hitting the pavement, and pain shot through my wrists.

A fist slammed into me, then another. I struggled to protect myself, but they were on me, shouting at me to stay down.

I didn't get it. If they wanted to make a show of bringing me in, fine. But did they have to hit me so—

Then it happened. I felt hot hell coursing through me.

It was like I'd been set on fire. My body shook, and I couldn't control it. The pain was all through me.

Die. I was going to die.

They were yelling at me to stay still, let them cuff me, give them my name. I could only shake and groan. They kicked me again and again, and I knew that if I didn't stop shaking they'd Taser me again and I'd be dead.

Finally I was cuffed and brought to a cruiser.

An officer said in my ear, "This one's for Prescott." Then he smacked my head into the car and pushed me into the backseat.

SLAP

The cops put me in Interview Room One and left me alone for a few minutes, wanting me to sweat. I put my head on the table and tried to rest. My whole body hurt from that goddamned Taser. They had no right to use that shit on me. I worked for them, didn't I?

Finally two cops came in. One was fat, his pants pulled up around his gut. The other was Asian with spiky black hair.

"Hello, Darren Lewis," said the Asian guy, reading my name off his clipboard.

My eyes flicked to his badge. "Chang. You the one who Tasered me?"

"No, our beat cops did. That's what happens when you run."

"I wouldn't have run if they'd been in a cop car or flashed some badges."

"From what I hear, you didn't give them a chance to talk to you," said Fattie. "You took off."

"If you had nothing to hide, why'd you run?" Chang asked.

"Why do you think? I thought I was gonna get shot."

Chang's eyes narrowed. "Why's that? Has your cover been blown?"

So Chang knew that I was an informant. That was a relief. Then why the hell did they beat on me like that?

"My cover's intact. But when the unmarked car came after me, I figured it was one of Tony's goons, or maybe the Bloods. I wasn't going to stand there while someone rolled down their window and shot me."

"We're onto you, Darren," Chang said. "You don't need to play innocent. We know you set up Prescott."

"That's bullshit. I'm his informant. We were—" I almost said "friends," but I knew they wouldn't buy it. "We were cool."

Chang's mouth twisted in disgust. "He trusted you, and you hung him out to dry."

"What the fuck are you talking about?"

"You CIs, you're all the same." Fattie sneered. "Snitches can't be trusted. I've seen it a million times. CI gives a tip or two and makes a quick buck, then turns on you. I bet you gave up every bit of information you knew about our operation, and convinced Walker that Prescott was his enemy. Did Walker give you a bonus for that?"

"If he knew I was a CI, I'd be dead by now."

"How do we know Walker didn't plant you?" Chang asked. "According to your file, you came to us."

"If you think I'd . . ." I didn't even know what to say. And then, suddenly, I did. "Check Prescott's cell phone. I called him last night and left a message saying he should watch out."

Chang didn't blink. "There weren't any messages on his phone. I checked myself."

"That's impossible. I know I left that message. You have to check again. Maybe he erased it."

A hand smacked the back of my head. I hadn't seen it coming, so I sprawled across the table like a rag doll, smacking my cheek against metal.

I told myself to stay calm. I wasn't going to give them the satisfaction of seeing me lose it. But as I stared at the cold metal table, I felt a rush of panic. Were they going to charge me as an accomplice to murder? I couldn't get locked up again. I couldn't.

"Don't think you're getting away with this, Darren." Chang loomed above me. "It's just a matter of time before we find evidence to put you away—as an adult this time, I promise you. You'll be eighteen before you see trial."

I lifted my head. "If you're done threatening me, I'd like to talk to Prescott's partner, Detective Kessler." I hoped I'd gotten the name right. Prescott had only mentioned his partner once, and it might've been a slip.

Chang exchanged a not-so-subtle glance with Fattie. "You're dealing with us, not Kessler. Got it?"

"Tell Kessler if he wants to bring down his partner's murderer, I'll help. Tell him he's gotta check the cell phone records."

"Tell *him*? Kessler's a woman, you dumbass." Fattie cackled. "Sounds like you and Prescott were really close."

"I take it you're not charging me. 'Cause if you are, then I'll need a lawyer."

"We're not charging you yet, Darren. But we will. Prescott was a good cop, but he never should've trusted you." Chang leaned close to me. "Did you know he had two babies at home? Babies that don't have a daddy anymore. Doesn't that tear you up?"

"Eleanor and Grace," I said quietly.

He got in my face. "What's that?"

"Eleanor and Grace. And yeah, I know they don't have a daddy no more. And it tears me up."

I glanced from one cop to the other. "If you want justice for Prescott, you'll stop dicking around and go after Diamond Tony hard. From what I see, Prescott was the only one in this department with the balls to do that."

This time I knew the slap was coming. And I didn't care.

HEADSPACE

When I got home, Kiki was watching *Dora* and Tasha was doing her nails on the couch. She swung around.

"Where have you been? It's your day to get Kiki. Noreen had to call me to come get him."

"Sorry." I was glad she hadn't heard that I'd been picked up. "I got a detention and forgot to call."

"Mom ain't gonna be happy about this. I won't tell her if you pick him up every day next week."

"Fine." And because I knew Kiki was listening, I said, "I like picking up Kiki."

I dropped my knapsack and threw my coat on a chair, then

went to see him. "Sorry, man. Hope you didn't miss me too much."

He was staring at the TV, riveted. I wondered if that Dora chick had some sort of mind control going on.

"Kiki? You're not mad at me, are you?"

He flicked his arm to shoo me away. He didn't seem mad. He just wanted to watch his show.

"Okay, little brother. I got you. I better go start my homework."

I went to my room and sat on my bed.

Prescott's protection had died with him. Now I had two enemies— the cops and the Walker gang. And no allies. How was I going to bring Diamond Tony down with the cops determined to bring *me* down?

Should I walk away, abandon my mission? If it was the only way to save myself from getting arrested again, I'd have to. Problem was, by now Tony would know that the cops had brought me in. What would he think if I just up and quit?

He could get suspicious and end me like he ended Prescott.

Unless . . .

Kessler. Maybe she would listen. I didn't need those other cops to help me contact her. I'd find a way to do it myself.

I turned on my computer. I'd bought it hot a few weeks ago. A necessary expense, since Tasha and Mom were always on the other one, and it was really slow.

I opened Google and typed in *Kessler Toronto Police Department*.

Score! The third entry that came up was her LinkedIn page, which she'd put up five months ago. It must mean she was looking for a new job. Not only was there contact information, but I could see where she'd worked over the last few years and where she graduated from college. Turned out she was from Vancouver.

I made some notes before calling her. I *had* to convince her to deal with me.

She answered on the first ring. "Kessler."

"This is Darren, Prescott's CI. I really need to talk to you."

There was a pause. "I don't know what you want, but I can't help you."

"I didn't sell him out to Diamond Tony. You have to believe me."

She sighed. "Look. Everybody's upset right now. If they didn't arrest you, they've got nothing on you. That's all I can say."

"Wait—please. I want to finish what I started. I'm already in with Tony Walker's operation, and it won't be easy to get out now. I need the cops to stay away from me. I can still help you get evidence on Diamond Tony."

"You were Ed's CI, and whatever deal you had with him is over. The department thinks you're involved in his murder. Even if they can't prove it, they're never going to work with you again."

"I spent two years in juvie because of Tony Walker. That's why I became a CI. Prescott understood. He said he had instincts about people. He knew right away he could trust me."

"Maybe I don't have his instincts. Why should I trust you?"

"I called Prescott about nine o'clock last night to warn him that he could be in danger. The cops that picked me up said there were no messages on his cell phone. Maybe Prescott got the message and erased it. There's got to be a way you can check it out."

"I'll do my best. How can I reach you?"

"This number. It's the secret cell phone Prescott gave me."

"Okay." She hung up.

I sat on my bed and said a little prayer for Kessler to clear my name. For all the good praying did—it had never helped me before.

THE BUZZ

A few minutes later, the intercom buzzed, making me jump.

"Darren!" Tasha called. "Some guy named Fry is downstairs!"

"Tell him I'll be right down," I shouted back.

Fry. It was one of Vinny's many nicknames. It came from nonstick frying pans, because charges never stuck to him.

"Who's Fry?" Tasha asked when I came out of my bedroom.

"A kid from school who's supposed to give me his history notes. Charges twenty bucks, but I should ace the test." At the mention of school, she lost interest and turned back to her manicure. I glanced at Kiki, who was still staring at the TV.

When I got downstairs, Vinny was waiting outside the building. For once, he wore a hoodie instead of his fur coat.

Vinny and I started to walk.

"We heard," he said. I figured *we* meant Diamond Tony and his executives. "How hard they lean on you?"

I snorted. "Same old shit. They promised they'd be watching us pretty good."

"Why'd they think they can lean on *you*?" Vinny didn't pull any punches.

"They saw me around and figured they'd try to spook me. Don't worry, Vinny. I gave them nothing. You know me."

"I do, soljah." He clapped a hand down on my shoulder. "What they say about the cop murder case? They got any ideas about it?"

It was as good as an admission that Diamond Tony was behind it. Not that I needed confirmation.

"They're saying it was a revenge murder. They think the cop who got killed pissed off DT. Sounded to me like they had nothing. But you know how it is. They'll be on us for a while. Point is, everybody needs to be careful."

"We'll be running a tight ship these next couple weeks until we can give the cops what they want."

"How you gonna do that?"

"South Side, Darren." There was that sly grin, the one that

had freaked me out last night. "We got peeps willing to testify that Andre made the call to kill the cop."

I was stunned, but raised my eyebrows, trying to look impressed. "Very nice. Hope it works out."

"It will."

"That'll be good for our man DT."

"Good for us all."

LAYERS

Hundreds of uniformed cops came out for Prescott's funeral. A picture of his grieving wife and his twin baby girls took up half a page in the *Star*. I brought the paper home with me, tore out the page, and tucked it under my mattress. I'd look at it in case I ever forgot what my mission was.

I spent every second of the next few days expecting the cops to make good on their threat and arrest me. Detective Chang was probably right—they'd charge me as an adult this time.

Maybe I'd even meet up with my old buddy Jongo.

Jessica sensed something was bothering me, though I kept denying it. She saw through me like no one else. My strategy was to avoid giving her the chance to ask questions. That meant more time sitting with friends at school or hanging out in the living room with Kendra. But I missed my alone time with Jessica.

It was a whole week until I heard from Kessler. I got home from my corner late one night to find that the secret cell had gotten several calls.

When I phoned her back, she picked up right away.

"I found the message you left on Ed's phone. The guys at the station know you weren't involved in his death."

Relief flooded through me. I sprawled backward on my bed. "How'd you find it? They told me it got erased."

"Don't be concerned with the details. Just be glad I found the message."

"Thanks for taking care of it."

"You were right about Ed. He had instincts about people. He'd have wanted me to check out your story. I suggest you call it quits, Darren. You've done some good, but you should move on. Get as far away from the Walker gang as possible. I'm sure it's what Ed would want."

"He wanted to see Tony's operation shut down. I'm not ready to end this. But if I don't have a contact in the PD, I'll have to."

"It's up to you, Darren. If you have information, I'm listening."

"I do have information."

"Go on."

"I will. But we've got to meet in person."

The sight of Kessler took me by surprise. On the phone, she sounded kind of tired, kind of old, but in person she was cute, with a curvy body. She had light brown skin and no makeup, making her look clean, *au natural*, and her hair was pulled back tightly, like a sexy librarian.

I bet Prescott noticed all of this too. Any red-blooded man would.

Kessler and I met at a vegan coffee shop downtown. She must've chosen it thinking that peeps from my neighborhood would never walk into a place like this. No doubt she was right.

Kessler was drinking funny-smelling green tea. She put an oatmeal square and a bottle of organic guava juice on my side of the table. I bet it cost ten bucks.

"Go ahead," she said. "It's gluten free."

I took a bite. It was good, but a little dry. "No offense, but I've never seen a granola cop. Prescott was all about the brownies."

She cracked a smile. "I tried to get him to lay off those things. So many empty calories." Her smile drained away. "I should've let him enjoy them."

There were a few seconds of silence. I finished the square, washing it down with the juice.

"Ed didn't tell me much about you," she said. "Just that he had a kid on the inside of the Walker gang. 'A kid who had a beef with them,' is what he said. He worked with a number of CIs over the years, but kept it as quiet as possible. The fewer people who knew, the better."

"Makes sense."

"Ed knew that going after the Walker gang was ambitious. And dangerous. One time he let on that he was worried for your safety."

"Really?"

"Yeah. But he said you were determined. I guess you and Ed were alike that way. So tell me, Darren. What's this intel you've got for me?"

"I'll tell you. But first I need to know that we trust each other. Quid pro quo, as they say. I need the truth about where my phone message went and why those cops told me it got erased. Why'd they lie about it?"

Kessler pursed her lips, discomfort written all over her face. She wouldn't make it undercover, that was for sure.

"It didn't get erased," she admitted. "Ed had two cell phones. The department didn't know about the second until I told them."

"So he had a second cell phone just for informants."

Her eyes darted to the window, then back to me. "I'm not saying more than that."

"Then I'm not either."

"He left it at my place," she said quietly.

Finally it clicked. They were more than just partners.

"He never got the message?" I asked.

She stared down at the table. "I heard it go off, but I didn't check the message. I wish to God I had. If he'd been on guard when he got out of the car that night . . ." She exhaled. "You can think what you want about me. It was complicated."

"I'm not thinking anything about you. I know all about complicated."

"So are you going to tell me this tip, or am I wasting my time?"

I glanced over my shoulders, just in case. No one was within earshot. "Diamond Tony is going to frame Andre of the South Side Bloods for Prescott's murder. Tony's got guys in the Bloods who are willing to testify that Andre ordered it."

"Do you have any details about what their story's going to be?"

"No, but Tony knows what sticks and what doesn't. Vinny— that's one of Tony's lieutenants—was sure that their plan was gonna work."

"God. The department might've bought it too."

"That's all I know," I told her. "You've got to take it from here."

"I will," she said, a steel edge in her voice. She wanted to put away Prescott's killer as much as I did.

STOP-LOSS

I could picture Diamond Tony smiling.

Andre down, check.

New suppliers, check.

Saturday morning I felt so depressed that I didn't want to get out of bed. It killed me that I might've had something to do with Tony's good fortune. If I hadn't tipped off Prescott about Pup or the Cash Stop, all of this might've played out differently.

My phone rang, and Jessica's number came up. I couldn't talk to her, not now.

I called White Chris. An hour later, I met him at Local's. When I got to the table, he did something he never did. I mean, *never*.

He hugged me.

"What was that for?"

White Chris sat down and looked at me over his basket of chicken wings. "I heard about the cop getting killed. I'm glad it wasn't you."

"Me too." It felt wrong saying it. Prescott's only mistake had been putting himself out there in front of the cameras, bringing all that attention to himself. If anyone was setting themselves up to get killed, it was me. Yet I was still living and breathing.

"I was his informant," I whispered.

White Chris's eyes widened.

"I'm in touch with his partner now. I told her that Tony is framing Andre of the South Side Bloods for the murder."

"So killing that cop was all part of his master plan."

"Right. The cops aren't listening to her, though. They're still going to charge Andre. Turns out he's got plenty of reasons to want Prescott dead. Prescott's been a pain in the ass to the Bloods for years. He even charged Andre a couple of years ago, but Andre got off on a technicality."

"Typical. The cops have to put someone away, even if he's not the real killer."

"And now Tony's hooked into the Bloods' suppliers. I don't know how he did it. He got everything he wanted. Revenge, supply, everything." I put up a hand. "Don't say 'I told you, he's smarter than you.' Just don't."

"I won't. It doesn't matter. The only thing that matters is what you do next."

"You think I should get out."

"I *thought* you should before. Now I *know* you should. Tony killed a cop, Darren. And not just any cop—your contact. That means he could've seen him meet with you."

"If he had, I'd be dead by now," I said. But it was still there, the gnawing fear in the pit of my stomach.

"For the first time in your life, you're a lucky bastard. Now get the hell out." He violently bit into a chicken wing to emphasize the point. "Look, if I saw you standing in the middle of the road with a Mack truck headed for you, I'd—"

"Okay."

He blinked. "Did you just say *Okay?*"

I was shocked, too. I couldn't quit. I'd come too far, seen too much. And now there was Prescott to avenge.

But none of that changed one simple fact: White Chris was right. I had to get out while I still could.

I knew what it meant to say I was getting out. It meant that I'd failed. It meant that everything I'd worked to achieve in the past few months had been a waste.

But it was like we'd learned in economics class—everybody has to have a point when you get out at all cost, no matter how much you've lost. A point where you save whatever assets you have left.

Even if the only asset you have left is your life.

"You're right," I said. "About everything. Now I have to figure out how to do it. Most people don't up and quit, especially with all the shit going down these days."

"Keep it simple. You can say that your mom heard about your dealing and threatened to kick you out."

I thought about it and nodded.

"You're doing the right thing, Darren."

But I wasn't sure that jumping ship and saving myself was the right thing. I only knew I wasn't ready to give up my life for this. Maybe my dad could do that, could give up his life for some cause bigger than he was. But I couldn't. I wasn't going to leave Kiki to grow up without me.

I didn't care what the right thing was anymore. I wanted to stay alive.

My Dad

My dad fought to keep the peace
And died a victim of war

One picture's all I have
Of him in his uniform
Growing up I needed
My dad, someone wise
Now I got no memories
None to love or to despise
A boy needs his dad
To show him the right way
How to handle the streets
And what game not to play
One picture's all I have
Of my dad, of my dad
One picture's all I have
And it's never been enough.

THE TWIST

How come we can't see stars in the projects?" Cam asked me. The sky was smoky black. Vinny was supposed to come by soon to make the last exchange of the night. That's when I planned to tell him my decision.

"All that pollution." I filled my lungs with cold air, then exhaled. "Hey, I got something to tell you."

"Then tell me."

"The other night I got into a fight with my mom. One of her friends spotted me out here and told her I was up to no good."

"Shi-it! What did you say?"

"What could I say? I pleaded no contest. She told me to pack my bags and get out."

"Ouch. Where'd you go?"

"I had nowhere to go. Couldn't show up at Jessica's and ask to crash there. Her parents would know something was up."

"So what'd you do?"

"I told my mom I'd get out of the biz."

"And she believed you?"

"It's the truth. I'm getting out."

He watched me for a minute, probably expecting me to burst out laughing. "You serious?"

"Dead serious. I'm not gonna get kicked out of my home for this, Cam. The whole time I was in juvie, I wanted to get back with my family. I'm not gonna blow it."

"Jeez. I thought you'd be a lieutenant one day."

"You did?"

"Yeah. Remember how Diamond Tony acted when he saw you at Vinny's? It was like he respected you. I figured that meant you were gonna move up."

"Thanks for saying that, Cam. But it don't matter now. It's not worth losing my family. They went through a lot while I was in juvie. And, to tell you the truth, I really don't want to get locked up again. Two years was enough."

"I hear that. But it'll be shitty without you. We had fun, huh?"

"Damn right." I went over, and we fist bumped. "We'll still hang. Hit a club or two."

"Fo sho."

I was surprised that Cam hadn't tried to talk me out of it, but I shouldn't have been. Maybe he knew I wasn't cut out for this. Maybe he thought he wasn't either. He'd been talking about doing his GED, after all.

Part of me wondered if I should try to talk Cam into quitting too. I wanted to see him do better, have a decent sort of life. But even if I could convince him, I didn't think Vinny would like both of us quitting at the same time. Better it just be me for now.

"Darren." I heard my name and spun around. The Vet had come up behind me, silent in the snow. He had that scary, zombie look going on, his skin mottled and colorless. I was surprised he knew my name, and I didn't like it.

"Haven't seen you in a while," I said, trying to be nice. "You want twenty?"

He stepped closer, reeking like garbage. "I want free."

"C'mon, man. It's too cold to be playing around."

"I ain't playing. But I know *you* been playing."

I made a face. "Huh?"

"I saw his picture in the paper."

An icy feeling gripped me. "I don't know what you're—"

"That cop who got killed. He was in the paper. I saw you with him."

"You're fucked up already," I said. "You obviously don't need any shit from us."

"I do. And I want it for free."

STUCK

There was no time to think, so I went with it. I pretended to take money from the Vet and slip it into my pocket. Then I made a sign to Cam.

"See ya next time, Darren," the Vet said, strolling over to Cam to collect his hit.

I watched him go. This had to be a nightmare. He couldn't have seen me with Prescott, could he?

Sure, he could have. The Vet didn't always hang out in this neighborhood. He probably panhandled all over the city.

He could put the word out about me so easily. Spread a rumor that I was a snitch. Or go up to some dealer and tell him what he saw. If Tony got suspicious, it could be enough to do me in.

I wished the free hit was all the Vet was after. But he'd said he would see me next time. That meant he was coming back for more, and if I wasn't here to supply him . . .

Every curse I knew shot through my brain.

I couldn't quit. Not now. Not before I found a way to deal with the Vet.

Vinny showed up soon after. When I saw his car pull up to the curb, it hit me that I was going to be twenty dollars short. Turning my back on Cam, I made a quick maneuver and replaced the missing twenty with one from my wallet. Good thing I had the cash on me.

I handed Vinny the money, and Cam gave back what we hadn't sold. Cam kept looking at me expectantly, but I gave a little shake of my head. He frowned, but seemed to get the picture.

Vinny didn't count the cash, but he could tell it was a fat wad. "We're back in business."

He slapped us five and strutted back to his car.

Cam turned to me. "You punked out or what?"

"Yeah. I got no other source of cash flow. I'm gonna have to get a job quick."

"What about your mama?"

I sighed. "I'll deal with my mama. Hope you got a spare couch in case I need to crash."

"It's yours if you need it, but it's got a couple of broken springs. Your sister's a wildcat."

I forced a laugh, but my stomach was in knots. The Vet knew my secret.

I couldn't get out now.

I was stuck in the game.

LUCK

Some people say there's no such thing as luck. I say there is. Mine's mostly bad.

I knew the Vet wouldn't hesitate to rat on me if I didn't supply him. Most fiends' brains were too fried to hold a conscience. They stole from their family and friends, neglected their kids, robbed shops, turned tricks—all to get their next hit. Why shouldn't he sell me out?

The Vet came back the next night and the night after that. Each time, I supplied him and covered the cost. The Vet never used to come by every night, but now that he had this sweet deal, he was making the most of it.

"Look, man, you're bleeding me dry," I said on the fourth night. "This is the last time."

He smiled, revealing horrible teeth. "Then say your goodbyes, Darren."

"No one will believe you."

"You sure about that?"

The next night he didn't come around, and I dared to hope I'd seen the last of him. But, of course, the Vet was back the following night. Seeing the smirk on his face, I could tell he was screwing with me. After I was done dealing, I didn't go home. Instead I walked north, up Jane Street. I'd been outside for hours and was bone cold. And yet I felt more suffocated than in those tiny cells in juvie where I could've sworn the walls were closing in.

It didn't matter how long I walked, I couldn't clear my head. I thought about telling Kessler my situation, seeing if she could get the Vet picked up and charged with possession. But I knew the cops didn't give a shit about crackheads like him. They always went right back to using once they got out. And even if they prosecuted him, it wouldn't solve my problem. The Vet could blab about me at any time, and snitching was just as bad in jail as it was on the outside.

Even if I kept supplying the Vet, he might talk anyway. He could brag about our arrangement when he was high; then I'd have more fiends to keep quiet. All I knew was, if anyone started calling me a snitch, it was only a matter of time before Tony took notice.

I heard my name and looked up, jarred out of my thoughts. It was stupid to be walking the streets so late without paying attention to my surroundings.

Then I heard my name again and saw her. Jessica hurried across the street. "What are you doing here?"

"Here" meant one block from Chaos and a lot of blocks from home. I'd wandered here without thinking. I must've meant to come this way, closer to her.

"You're done for the night," I said, stating the obvious.

"Of course." She searched my eyes. "I called you twice today."

"Sorry, I didn't get a chance to call you back."

"Are you all right?"

"Yeah." It was another lie. I hated lying to her.

She didn't buy it. "You're freezing. Let's go inside, okay? I could use some hot chocolate."

I nodded and followed her to the Arab diner around the corner.

We ordered at the counter. As we waited, we didn't speak. My ears stung from the cold. The heat of the place started to thaw my skin but did nothing to melt the ice block inside me.

We settled into our seats. She waited for me to take a sip, then asked, "What's going on?"

I was about to give some lame excuse, but she held up her hand. "Don't lie to me, Darren. Please."

I paused. I didn't want to lie.

"Tell me one thing," she said. "Are *we* okay?"

"Yeah, we're okay." *Until I get killed*, I didn't add. I could almost hear the gun going off inside my head.

"Does it have to do with work?" she asked.

I nodded. "You don't want to know, Jessica. Trust me. You should stop asking questions."

Suddenly she grabbed my hand across the table. "Let's go."

"Where we going?"

"Somewhere private."

We caught a cab to her building and took the elevator to the top floor. There was a rec lounge that residents could use for birthday parties but rarely did. It was totally old-school, with faded flowery wallpaper. The pool table was scratched up, and the dart board didn't have any darts. But none of that mattered since the couches were soft.

The lounge was locked, but Jessica had a key, which she'd swiped from the landlord's office years ago. We'd been up here a few times before. Sometimes she brought her laptop and we watched movies. Or we made out. Or just sat here holding hands, listening to music with shared earbuds.

We sat down on the couch, and she turned to me. "Talk."

Maybe I should. I'd told myself that lying to her was keeping her safe, but I wasn't so sure anymore. If the Vet ratted me out and Tony came after me, she could get caught in the crossfire. She deserved the truth so that she could decide for herself if being with me was worth the risk. And if she decided it wasn't, I couldn't blame her.

"All right." I was finally done lying to her, and it was a relief. "I'm not in the game for the reasons you think. I've been informing to the cops."

She stared at me. "You're working with the *cops*?"

"Yeah." I knew she might judge me for it, but I still knew I could trust her. "We wanted the same thing: to see Diamond Tony locked up."

"Why?"

"I lost two years of my life because of Tony. I was just a lookout, but the second we were busted, I got stuck with the package and the jail time."

"You want revenge."

"Yeah, but it's not just about that. Tony controls this whole neighborhood, and it's got to stop. It's like this . . . terror monarchy."

"And I bought your story about wanting to make some money." She shook her head. "I kept asking myself why you'd go back to the business after two years in juvie. Now I know." Suddenly her eyes went wide. "Oh my God—Tony didn't find out about you, did he?"

"No. Not yet."

I told her about the Vet blackmailing me. As I spoke, tears formed in her eyes.

"You've got to run, Darren. It's too risky for you to stay here. The Vet could talk anytime."

"There's no running. Not while I still have family here. Tony wouldn't hesitate to use them to get to me."

"Can't the cops protect you?"

"I don't see how. If they arrest the Vet, he'll definitely talk."

She put her face in her hands. "Why did you have to do this? It was a crazy idea."

"I thought I could pull it off. Figured it was worth the risk. So many people have died because of Diamond Tony. Makes me sick that everybody thinks he's a hero."

"I know. I feel the same way." She hesitated. "There's something I never told you. My family swore me to secrecy, but it's been eating away at me."

"You can tell me anything."

"Diamond Tony killed Valerie."

My mouth fell open. "*What?* I thought it was a car accident."

"It was. Because she was high out of her mind."

I couldn't believe it. Valerie, high out of her mind? She'd been a straight-A student, a totally together person.

"Valerie was wound up so tight, you know? Sometimes she'd smoke weed to relax. But Diamond Tony started giving away free hits of Diamond Dust to the stoners. She tried it once, and that was it. She was hooked."

"Damn. I'm sorry, Jessica." I hugged her.

"Her parents didn't know she was using. When the police told them there were drugs in her system, they didn't believe it." She sighed. "But I knew. So did her brother. We'd finally convinced her to go to rehab. I was making phone calls to find a place that would take her. Then the accident happened." She took a deep breath. "If I'd been able to check her in somewhere right away, she'd still be alive. Even if I'd taken her to a psych ward, just to get her off the streets . . ."

"You did everything you could."

"It wasn't enough."

"It's not your fault. Diamond Tony's the one who's responsible."

"I know." Her arms tightened around me. "I can't lose you, too, Darren. The Vet could be telling people he saw you with that cop. What are you going to do?"

"I'll figure it out."

I had to. My life depended on it.

BLACKMAIL

White Chris lived on a tree-lined street with big old houses and Lexus SUVs. He thought of his neighborhood as quiet and boring, but I didn't see it that way. It would be perfect for Kiki. The park across the street was clean and had all the newest play equipment. You didn't see dealers on the corners or have to duck drive-bys. I planned to move my family here one day . . . if I didn't get myself killed first.

White Chris answered the door in baggy sweatpants and a wifebeater that showed off his scrawny arms. We went downstairs to shoot pool. His basement had shag carpets, comfy furniture, and hip-hop blaring from the Bose. His production equipment took up half the room. It was all top of the line, thanks to his parents' deep pockets. They'd bought it for him when he was released from juvie to keep him out of trouble. I knew he'd have stayed out of trouble anyway.

"Thanks for letting me come over," I said.

He tossed me a cue. "You didn't get out of the game, did you?"

I shook my head. "One of the fiends is blackmailing me. He saw me with that detective and figured it out. Said he'd put the word out if I didn't supply him. So I've been giving him a free hit every night."

"That's fucked up." He arranged the balls in the triangle. "You want to break?"

I did, slamming the white ball so hard it popped off the table.

He took his shot from the scratch line, sinking a solid in a side pocket. His next shot was off by an inch. "You don't have too many options."

"I know."

"You have to deal with him."

"How? Give him a plane ticket to Vegas?" But I knew what he was going to say.

"Take him out." White Chris chalked his cue. "I know it's the last thing you want to do. But it's you or him. Who do you want it to be?"

"Neither. I was thinking about paying him off."

"That might work for a while."

But it wouldn't solve the problem. We both knew that.

"Killing someone's Diamond Tony's MO, not mine," I said. "Let's take it off the table."

"You're so noble. I'm sure they'll think of something nice to write on your tombstone." He took another shot, this time landing two solids in a row. His next shot sank a striped ball, so I took over.

"I'm not trying to be noble. I'm not even saying he doesn't deserve it. I just don't think I could kill him."

"You could if you had no choice."

"There has to be another way."

"Then get someone else to do it. Some fiend who could never prove that you hired him."

"Yeah, and he'd probably blackmail me too."

"I'll break it down for you, bro. If you were on a battlefield and the Vet was holding up a machine gun, would you shoot? Because he's basically got a gun pointed at your head."

I knew he was right. But still.

"Look, the Vet's playing with fire here. If he's a real war vet, he should know that. Kill or be killed."

I was about to take another shot when it hit me. "I can handle him the way I handled Jongo."

He raised his eyebrows. "You're gonna let him stab you?"

"No. I'll let him seal his own fate."

NO BLUFF

That night, the Vet walked up to me with that same jittery eagerness he'd had all week.

"Our arrangement is over," I said, point-blank.

"Oh yeah? I wonder what Mr. Kingpin will say about that."

The Vet had no idea that blackmailing me was putting his life at risk too. That was about to change.

"I'm going to make you a deal, Vet."

He made a face. "Dinner and a movie? Me and you?"

"I'm only going to say this once, so listen up. If you bother me again, I'll tell Tony you gave me these." I pulled two fake tens out of my pocket and held them up. I'd gotten conned with them a few summers ago when I'd sold a kid a video game. I was glad I'd hung on to them. "Any guess what he'll do when he finds out you paid with counterfeits?"

The Vet looked startled.

"You can sing about me all you want, Vet. When I show these bills to Tony, you'll have a bullet in your head so fast that nothing you say will matter. That's if you're lucky. If you're not, it'll be a baseball bat instead of a bullet."

He shrugged. "If I'm dead, you're dead. Now, where's my hit?"

"Not unless you've got money for me."

He went up to Cam. "I want my hit!"

Cam glanced at me. I shook my head and held up the fake bills. "He tried to pay with counterfeits."

"He's lying!" the Vet shouted. "I didn't give him nothing. I get my hits for free."

Cam crossed his arms. "I never knew Darren was so generous."

"It's because I know his secret."

"Good for you," Cam said. "Now get out of here."

The Vet didn't move. "Darren is a snitch! A snitch!"

"Shut the fuck up," I said, taking a step closer to him.

The Vet turned to Cam. "I bet you're in on it too! Did you snitch to that cop—the one who got killed?"

"I told you, get out of here." Cam moved beside me.

The Vet lunged at Cam, grabbing at his coat pocket. Cam tried to dodge him but stumbled backward. With surprising speed, the Vet pounced, knocking him to the ground. I tried to pull the Vet off Cam, but he was thrashing like crazy.

Cam screamed. Then I saw the knife.

I slammed my foot into the Vet's side, partially dislodging him. The Vet bucked, slashing wildly. Cam grabbed the Vet's arm, and they fought for control of the knife.

Suddenly the Vet shrieked and fell to the ground.

Cam scrambled to his feet, clutching his shoulder. He gasped for breath. "Fuck! He stabbed me!"

I could see Cam was bleeding. "We need to get you to a hospital."

Cam nodded, mouth twisting in pain. "What about him?"

Blood gushed from the Vet's throat. I bent over him, heard gurgling sounds. I took off my jacket, and pressed my hoodie against his neck.

"We'll call nine-one-one," I said. "But we can't leave him at our corner."

Cam pointed to a bus stop a few yards away. "We leave him over there."

"Okay." I took out my cell. My hand was shaking. White Chris's words came back to me. *It's you or him. Who do you want it to be?*

There was a gasp. The Vet's arms had gone limp by his sides, and his eyes were blank. I'd seen that look before.

"He's dead." I got up.

Cam went pale. "W-what are we gonna do? I didn't mean to kill him."

I glanced down at the knife, the blood, trying to process what had just happened.

My mind switched into high gear. I scanned the area and saw no witnesses. "The alley. Hurry."

I dragged the Vet's body into the alley. Cam helped with his good arm. He was breathing hard, swearing over and over.

"We call Vinny," I said. "He'll know what to do."

"Wait—what are we going to tell him?" Cam asked, his voice shaky. "I mean, it was self-defense. You saw it. Tony's not gonna blame me for this, right?"

"Of course not. I'll tell Vinny what happened and he'll explain it to Tony." I tried to speak as calmly as possible, tried to dissolve Cam's panic even in the midst of my own. "The Vet started this, not us. He tried to pull one over on Tony. Here's the proof." I took out the fake bills.

"Then he went all crazy and started calling you a snitch and—"

Cam broke off, his face sobering. "Maybe we shouldn't mention that."

"Yeah, there's no point." I studied Cam. "You know that was bullshit, right?"

Cam nodded. He believed me. I thought he did, anyway.

I said into the phone, "Vinny, we got a situation."

NO PROBLEM

Turned out the death of a customer wasn't a problem as long as the body was properly dealt with.

And deal with it they did.

I rolled over and glanced at the clock. It was 10:36 a.m. Too early to wake up, considering I'd gotten home at five a.m. I turned over and buried my head in the pillow, trying to go back to sleep. That way I wouldn't have to remember.

But I remembered every detail.

Vinny had called the Cuz—two cousins, Remy and Tyrell—who did dirty work for Tony. They were goons, enforcers, like Pup had been. Whether it was a murder or a crime scene cleanup, if the job involved blood, you could bet the Cuz would be there.

I wished I hadn't been there to see it, wished I hadn't wondered how many times the Cuz must have disposed of bodies before.

I was glad Cam wasn't there to watch. Vinny had dropped him off at the hospital, where he got stitched. When I spoke to him a couple of hours later, he'd calmed down.

My cell buzzed. I groaned and grabbed it off the night table. It was Jessica, I saw with relief.

Wanna come over?

I texted back: *Thanx but I'm not feeling good today. Should stay home.* There'd be nothing better than to hang out with Jessica, but I knew she'd ask what was going on with the Vet. I wasn't ready to answer her.

She replied right away. *Take care. C U soon. xox*

I wasn't sure what was worse: the horror of what I'd seen last night, or the fact that I felt no regret about it. Shouldn't I feel bad that a man was dead, even a pathetic one like the Vet?

But the truth was, from the moment I saw the body slip beneath the black water of the Humber River, I felt nothing but relief. The Vet was gone and my secret was safe.

For now.

THE UGLY

Monday morning. I'd hoped school would be a distraction from my thoughts, but no such luck. By the time I showed up to Filimino's class, I was ready to get lost in the beats. I rapped inside my head:

> You can't wash off the ugly
> The stain of this game
> You carry it with you
> You'll never be the same
> It's a disease inside you
> Taking over your being
> You see all these people
> Go from normal to fiends.

Ricky tapped me on the shoulder, killing my flow. "I've been working on some new lyrics," he said.

Great. I wasn't in the mood to deal with him right now, but I didn't have a choice. "What kind of beat do you need?"

"Anything. I'll make it work."

"Okay." I put on a generic beat. "Go for it, then."

As usual, Ricky waited too many beats before starting. Just when I was getting really annoyed, he went, "Greatness is the aim/When you get into the game/The deals get done/The money, you get some/People running scared/But the kingpin has a plan/ He rules over the streets/Don't mess with Diamond Man."

He looked at me for approval.

What was he trying to do, rap like a gangster? He had no clue what Tony was made of. No clue about the game.

"What do you think?" he asked eagerly.

"I think you should rap about what you know. About your life. Not this gangster shit."

His face fell. "My life's too boring to rap about. But I could rap about yours."

I gritted my teeth, telling myself to be patient with the kid. There was a time when I'd been just like him—innocent, stupid. A time when I'd thought working for Diamond Tony meant a chance at an exciting life.

"Your life is boring? Well, I spent two years in juvie. Now, that's so boring you want to blow your brains out."

"Yeah, but . . ."

"But what?"

"Now you're back in the game, right?"

I loomed over him. "You keep asking questions like that and people will start talking about you. Thinking maybe you're a snitch or something. And you know what the Diamond Man does to snitches?"

Ricky swallowed and bent his head. I'd finally gotten through to the kid.

At lunch I stayed in the music room. That's where Jessica found me.

"I thought you weren't at school today. I was really worried." She wrapped herself around me.

"I'm sorry. I should've found you."

"You okay?"

I wasn't sure I knew the answer.

"Did the Vet come back?" she asked in a whisper, though we were alone in the room.

"Yeah. I told him that if he didn't back off, I'd tell Tony he gave me fake money. He got spooked."

"So he's going to leave you alone?"

I nodded.

"Thank God." She sighed with relief and hugged me.

I was tempted to tell her the truth, to get the ugliness off my chest. But I couldn't do that to her.

I squeezed Jessica tight. She was like an anchor keeping me grounded. How the hell had everything gotten so out of control?

GOING FOR A RIDE

Friday night Cam and I finished another cold shift. When Vinny approached to collect the stuff, I knew something was wrong. His swagger wasn't the same. He was edgy.

We did the usual exchange.

Vinny took a deep breath. "Darren, you gotta come with me. Tony wants to see you."

Panic shot through me. "N-now?" I couldn't help but stutter. Should I run?

"Yes, now. Let's go."

I glanced at Cam. He gave me an awkward wave and headed toward home. Had he talked? Had he told Tony that the Vet said I was a snitch?

Don't run, I told myself. The meeting could be about something else. If I ran, I'd look guilty. And what was the point? Tony could still get to my family, like he got to Pup's brother.

We went to Vinny's car. I got in and was about to buckle my seat belt, but decided not to. I might be better off if we got into an accident.

"What's Tony want to talk to me about?" I asked.

Vinny started the car. "He didn't say."

For all I knew, he was driving me to my death.

I should've run. Why didn't I run? I could've hauled it back to my apartment and called 911. Kessler would have protected me and my family. At least, she would've tried.

"You heard about Donut?" Vinny asked as he pulled onto the road.

"Yeah." Of course I'd heard about Donut. Everybody had. He was one of Tony's executives, and he'd gotten shot outside a club Tuesday night. "He okay?"

"He'll pull through. But he might not be able to walk again."

"Damn." Like I gave a shit about whether Donut walked or not. I just wanted to survive the next hour.

Maybe it had been a mistake to stay on after the Vet had been killed. I'd thought I should wait a couple more weeks before quitting. Cam had seemed traumatized by what'd happened, and I'd wanted to stay close by in case he was tempted to talk.

Maybe he *had* talked.

Dread rose inside me, and I tried to squash it down. I was being stupid. Diamond Tony wouldn't murder someone this way, would he? He'd catch them off guard in a parking lot or an alley, not send one of his lieutenants to pick him up. Anyone could see us driving together.

Then again, anyone who saw us wouldn't talk.

I prayed we were going somewhere public, but when Vinny stopped the car, my stomach dropped. We were parked in front of a row of town houses that were splattered with gang graffiti. The whole block was dark and deserted.

We got out of the car, and Vinny led me toward a town house with boarded-up windows. "Somebody live here?" I asked.

"Nah. It's a place we use sometimes."

To kill people? Oh God.

I followed him inside. When I caught the door behind him, it felt as though it could fall off the hinges. We walked down a dingy hallway that looked like a future crime scene. I just hoped I wasn't going to be the crime.

"There's something you should know about this place," Vinny said, stopping in front of another door. "It surprises you."

He did a series of knocks and the door opened. The Cuz were standing there. I froze.

"Come on in," one of them said, and I forced myself to move forward.

When we walked in, I hung back, as if standing behind Vinny would protect me from whatever was coming. Vinny shoved his hands in his pockets like he wasn't sure what to do either.

We were in a posh living room set up with leather furniture, a minibar, and a sound system. Sitting around the room were Diamond Tony and three of his executives—Marcus, Kamal, and Pox.

"Soljahs." Marcus stood up and bumped fists with us. "Darren, my man. Good night out there?"

"Yeah." It came out as a croak. My mouth was bone dry. "Business is great."

From his chair, I saw Diamond Tony nod.

"I guess you're wondering why we brought you here tonight," Marcus said.

"A little." My voice wavered.

Marcus smiled. The whole room could smell my nerves. "We have a matter to discuss, you see. One that has to do with you and Vinny."

Vinny looked like a deer in the headlights. This was catching him by surprise too.

"Sit down," Marcus said. "Sit down and relax."

Relax. Yeah, right. Vinny and I sat down on the nearest couch.

Tony took over. "Tonight's a big night for both of you. Your lives are gonna change."

I heard a gulp. I wasn't sure if it came from Vinny or me.

Tony said to Vinny, "I'm inviting you to become an executive. Donut won't be coming back. It was our unanimous decision that you should replace him."

"Shut up!" Vinny jumped off the couch and pumped his fist. Then he sat down and composed himself. "It's an honor. I'd be proud to be an executive."

Diamond Tony turned to me. "Darren. I've heard nothing but solid things about you. You been loyal and dependable. And you're cool under pressure. Which is why I'm promoting you to lieutenant."

I smiled. He wasn't going to kill me.

"I think you'll find it very rewarding," Tony added.

My relief suddenly switched to panic. A lieutenant? Could I say no without pissing him off? It hadn't exactly been an offer—it sounded more like an order.

"Got nothing to say?" Diamond Tony said.

"I'm surprised, but . . . it's an honor," I said, borrowing Vinny's words.

Diamond Tony's mouth moved in a fraction of a smile. Then he got up and slapped hands with both of us. "Congrats, soljahs."

The other executives congratulated us too. I thanked everybody, but I was totally stunned. As for Vinny, he was so excited that he couldn't sit still. Champagne was passed around, and the group broke into different conversations.

Vinny leaned over to me. "Sorry to scare you there. I was feeling bad for you. Last time Tony made me bring someone here, he left in a body bag."

I choked down the champagne.

The next few hours were dizzying, and not just because somebody kept refilling my glass. It felt like I'd been eavesdropping outside a doorway for months and now I'd finally been let into the conversation. They talked business. They talked about Andre rotting in prison. They talked about the next step in the plan for vengeance against the Bloods. They talked about their baby mamas and their naggy mamas.

They treated me like . . . not an equal exactly, but maybe a little brother.

Girls arrived at some point. They were classy, not skanky—you could always tell by the perfume. One of them ended up on my lap. She told me she was mine for the night, for whatever I wanted. But she wasn't the one I wanted. So I passed her off to Vinny, who said two was better than one.

I got home after sunrise. Some driver took me, but when I woke up the next afternoon, I didn't remember much more than that. I spent an hour in the bathroom, my stomach churning and my mind reeling.

I was in.

THE LIEUTENANT

Over the next forty-eight hours, I realized two things:

The stakes were higher than ever.

And there was no going back. When Diamond Tony made you an offer, you didn't turn it down.

"You start and finish the day at the stash house," Marcus explained my first day on the job. "We give you the money and the product, and you distribute it to your dealers. You check in on them a few times, see if they need any re-ups. Then you collect and drop it off at the stash house, where one of us execs will count it right away."

"So this is the stash house," I said, surveying the grimy walls.

"It is today. It'll change soon. We used to change it every couple of weeks, but Tony's taking extra precautions. We gotta stay a step ahead of the cops."

I nodded, thinking that I could bring a raid on this place anytime I wanted. It would give the cops a sweet photo op, but I doubted Diamond Tony would stop by a stash house to count his money anytime soon.

I'd called Kessler yesterday and told her about my promotion to lieutenant. After several beats of silence, she'd asked, "Are you sure you still want to do this?"

I wasn't sure about anything. But there was no point in telling her how close I'd come to quitting. It wasn't an option anymore. "I'm doing it. We're going to put away Prescott's killer."

"It's not 'we,' Darren. Don't forget that. I'll do whatever I can to help, but you're not a CI anymore. You're on your own out there."

She didn't need to remind me.

Marcus's deep voice brought me back to the present. "Wallop will be here soon to train you. He's the lieutenant who does the southwest. Tony's moving him to the northeast. You're gonna take over for him."

It took me a minute to process that. *The southwest? The busiest and the most dangerous corners, right smack in the middle of Blood/ Walker territory?* "You're kidding me."

He gave me a flat look. "I don't kid."

It was true. Marcus had no sense of humor. "I thought you'd want someone with more experience there."

Judging by Marcus's expression, I wasn't owed an explanation. "Tony's decision, not mine. You want to take it up with him?"

I shook my head. "No, I'm cool with it."

Wallop showed up soon after. He was short with a fat head and satellite-dish ears. I couldn't picture him walloping anyone without getting flattened.

"You can follow me around today," he said as we got into his car, an old Camry littered with fast-food wrappers and empty bottles. "Tomorrow you're on your own. You got a car?"

"No."

"Tony's got a few beaters like this you can use. Cars that don't attract attention. Marcus will hook you up. I keep my Camaro at home, see. Gotta keep it spotless for the ladies."

Yeah, right. Wallop must be *real* popular with the ladies what with his big head and Dumbo ears.

As he drove, he went over some rules of being a lieutenant. No business talk on cell phones. No dealing directly with customers. No using a GPS in the car or writing anything down. No shop talk with anyone but lieutenants or execs. When Wallop was done, he didn't bother to ask if I had questions; he just turned up the music.

It thumped through the car, rattling the windows as we cruised down the freeway.

I turned it down. "So why are you switching to the northeast?"

"They need me there." He turned the music back up.

That was bullshit and he knew it. The northeast was the quietest area of Tony's territory. I wished I knew why a newbie like me was being put on the most dangerous corners. I hoped it was because Tony thought I was tough enough to handle them, not because I was the most dispensable.

It wasn't long before I figured it out.

We stopped by the first corner, where Wallop stocked two street dealers, Busy and Steve. They were ranting about a confrontation they'd had with some Bloods last night. Wallop egged them on. He started talking war and guns and revenge and how they were gonna make everybody pay.

When we hit the second corner, Wallop supplied Two-Bit and P-Free with product, along with a totally exaggerated version of what had happened with Busy and Steve the night before. It was clear what was going on. Wallop was a hothead and an instigator. What these corners needed was a cooler. Somebody who knew that Tony called the shots and nobody else. Somebody who knew that street dealers had to stay on their game, not get caught up in the turf war.

It made perfect sense. I was the cooler.

Later that night, I called my dealers together. We met at the stash house once all the money had been taken elsewhere. I asked Marcus to stick around to give me extra street cred.

"Things are gonna change on the southwest side," I told them. "Tony's put me in charge now."

They weren't impressed. It didn't help that I was younger than most of them.

"I don't want to dis my man Wallop, but I'm gonna do things different. First of all, I'm switching you around. You're gonna work with different partners from now on."

That got them riled up. Steve started cursing. "Why you gotta do that?"

"Seems to me like you're all getting too comfortable out there, and I don't like it." I told them the new pairs and their locations.

"I only work good with Steve," Busy said. "We got a system going. I can't work with P-Free."

P-Free glared at him. "You got a problem with me?"

"This ain't open to negotiation," I said. "Tony told me to get the job done, and that's what I'm doing. If you have a problem with me, you can take it to Tony."

At the mention of Tony's name, everybody went quiet.

That was the thing about being a lieutenant. When I spoke, I was representing Tony. It gave my words a lot of weight. I felt powerful.

I went over some new rules. Most of them were about staying out of trouble. Don't carry guns. Don't mess with the neighborhood mamas. Don't talk back to the cops. Don't start anything with the Bloods.

"Tony and his executives are dealing with the Bloods," I said, and Marcus nodded. "If you start something on the street, you're getting in their way. Do you hear me?"

The guys grudgingly agreed, but I could tell they were pissed off. If they weren't so afraid of Tony, I bet they'd be spitting in my face right now.

I didn't care. I didn't need them to like me, just to follow my rules. The rules were for their survival.

And mine.

The Streets

There's a pounding in my head
A hammer in my chest
I gotta rise to the duty
Gotta do what's best
Every night on the streets
I hear a clock ticking away
Bloods could attack anytime
Will I live another day?

MAKING SENSE

D arren? Aren't you going to school?" Mom shouted.

I checked the clock. *Shit.* I was going to be late.

I swung my legs over the side of the bed, resting my head in my palms. Getting home at three in the morning and then waking up for school was crazy. But I couldn't hurry home to bed when all the guys were out partying. I had to be a lieutenant *and* act like one.

I took a quick shower, threw on some clothes, grabbed my knapsack, and ran out the door. "Bye, baby," Mom said cheerfully. She'd obviously seen the cash I'd left on the table.

The morning was cold and icy. I almost wiped out twice on my way to the bus stop. It was just me and a lady in a wheelchair. Great. It was gonna take ten minutes for her to get on the bus, making me even later. I wished I had one of Tony's beater cars—driving to school would be way quicker. But they were only for business. One of these days I'd buy a car of my own.

When I finally got to school, the bell was ringing, ending first period. At least I wouldn't have to walk in late to my second class. I caught sight of Jessica, who did a double take when she saw me. I hadn't phoned her all weekend, and I'd replied to her text messages with just a couple of words. She'd be wondering what the hell was going on.

"Jessica," I called out, going up to her. "We should talk. Meet me in the north stairwell at eleven forty-five."

She nodded, frowning.

I went to my class on the third floor, darting in the door right before the bell. Ms. Stark was putting up study notes for next week's test. Good. I didn't have to think or process information, I just had to write. I hadn't even had time for my choco-latte, which was probably part of the reason my head ached. The other part was all those drinks at the Velvet Room with the lieutenants.

When I got to the stairwell at eleven forty-five, the rush of students had already gone by, and Jessica was standing under the stairs. She gazed up at me, and the expression on her face said it all. "You're not getting out, are you?"

"It's gotten more complicated."

"Once the Vet stopped bothering you, you should've quit right away."

"I had to wait for the right time. And then Friday night, Tony promoted me to lieutenant."

"*What?* Oh my God." For a second, I thought she might pass out. "And you agreed?"

"You don't say no to Tony."

"So there's no way out anymore. Is that what you're saying?"

"I can't tell Diamond Tony I'm not cut out for the job. He knows I am."

"You *are?*"

"You know what I mean. It's business. Anyway, I've got the feeling I'm where I'm supposed to be. I have more access now. I can learn a lot about his operation."

She was gobsmacked. "You're in even more danger than before. Can't you see that?"

"I don't really have a choice. I have to make the best of the situation."

"Every minute of the last two days I was hoping you'd call to tell me you were out. You have to find a way, Darren. You have to."

"Jessica." I couldn't believe what I was about to say, but as soon as I'd been promoted, I'd known what I had to do. "Don't take this the wrong way, but I think we should take a break until this is all over. It's too dangerous. If I get targeted . . ."

"No, Darren." She put a palm against my cheek. "I'm with you. No matter what."

I shook my head. "It's not a good idea. If Tony finds out what I'm doing, you're guilty by association. He could come after you." But even as I said it, I squeezed her closer.

"I told you, I don't care."

"I care. But—oh, fuck it." I kissed her. She kissed me back.

Jessica was with me. It was the only thing that ever made sense.

TOGETHER

We cut school that afternoon and went back to my place. Some things couldn't be denied.

I took her to my bedroom and we held each other for a long time. I didn't try to touch her more than that, but holding back just burned me up more. Then she told me she wanted me to touch her. Needed me to.

Hours later, we picked up Kiki from daycare. As soon as he saw Jessica, he raced into her arms. The sight of them together made my chest tighten.

We were a family.

I hoped that would never change.

GAME ON

A month went by. It was school by day, lieutenant by night, and Jessica whenever possible. February turned into March, and there were a lot of springlike days, but I wasn't thanking Mother Nature. The neighborhood had come out of their homes, and people were hanging around on porches, doorsteps, and street corners. I had to be ultracareful—any group of guys I walked by could be Bloods waiting to spot one of Tony's lieutenants.

Kessler called every few days on the secret cell. She was different from Prescott; though she asked me questions about Tony's operation, she never pushed me to dig deeper. As much as she wanted to put Diamond Tony away, she didn't want me taking any extra risks. I bet if it was up to her, she'd rather have me out of the game than supplying her with information.

But it was too late for that.

I'd finally found my groove as a lieutenant. It was all about problem solving. You got customers being a nuisance. You got loudmouthed mamas trying to shove the dealers off their corners. You got cops scoping the neighborhood. As soon as you fixed one problem, another cropped up. And just when you thought you had it all under control, you were proven wrong.

Like when I found two of my dealers in an alley, beaten bloody.

"They took everything," Busy said, cradling his arm and moaning with pain.

I crouched down beside P-Free. He was out cold.

"Is he dead?" Busy was panicked.

"No."

I called 911. Tony wouldn't like it, but P-Free was in bad shape. I wasn't going to risk him dying.

"Who did this?" I asked Busy.

"Don't know."

"Do you think they were Bloods? Were they wearing colors?"

"No colors. They were all in black. Pantyhose over their faces."

The ambulance was there five minutes later. I knew the cops

wouldn't be far behind. I helped Busy up. We had to leave the scene before they arrived.

Busy leaned on me heavily as I walked him home. I dropped him off in the lobby of his building, stuffing his pay into his pocket.

Then I headed for the stash house. It was a town house five blocks north of Busy's building. Sometimes the place was a crack house, but whenever Tony wanted to use it, his guys pushed the squatters out, cleaned it up a bit, and moved in for a few days.

The house was under guard, of course. Three guys were on the front porch, two in the back. They acted like they were chillin', but they watched anyone who came within twenty feet of the place like hawks. By now they knew me, so when I came up, they let me right in.

Kamal, one of the executives, was inside counting cash. When he saw me, he gave a grim nod. "I heard."

It had just happened, and he already knew. That showed how good Tony's pipeline was. He knew all the neighborhood events in real time.

"Did they recognize who jumped them?" Kamal asked.

"No."

"Must be Bloods."

"Maybe, but—"

He gave me a look that shut me up. I had the feeling it was going to be the Bloods whether there was proof or not.

The door burst open behind me, and a gust of cold air came in as Tony entered with Marcus and Pox.

"How much did they get away with?" Tony barked at me.

"Couple hundred, tops. I'd done a pickup an hour before."

"Blood motherfuckers messing with my corner. Cops crawling all over the place." He paced the room.

"I had to call nine-one-one." I was more afraid of what I held back from Tony than what I told him. He could see anything as a deception. "If P-Free died, we'd have even more cops coming around."

Diamond Tony inhaled sharply, but he didn't say anything. Pissed as he was, he knew it was the right call.

Eventually the rest of the lieutenants showed up to make their drop-offs. Everybody talked revenge, war, murder. Tony waved his hand, which meant the discussion was over. He would retaliate, but he wasn't going to tell us how.

When the lieutenants were done for the night, we went to Chaos. I was surprised that Jessica was working. Usually she only worked weekends, but she must've picked up a shift. I went over to her and gave her one helluva kiss.

The guys cheered and snickered when I sat down at our table.

"Last time I touched a waitress like that, I got slapped," Wallop said, taking a swig of beer.

"She's my girlfriend."

"Looks serious," Ray-go said. He and Abdul were the lieutenants who'd been at the mall with Vinny when we'd encountered the Bloods. Ray-go was as clean-cut as they come, while Abdul seemed to have a new tattoo every time I saw him.

"Darren's gonna give her something serious when she's done her shift, all right." Abdul pounded fists with Ray-go.

"Why wait till she's done? That's what the VIP coatroom is for." Wallop smirked. "She's fire hot, that one."

It was just as well that Jessica was working the other end of the club—I hated her anywhere near the VIP tables. On the whole, the lieutenants weren't bad, though. They talked tough, a lot like the guys in juvie. But unlike in juvie, these guys had my back. Diamond Tony's lieutenants were loyal—to him and to each other.

"The Bloods are gonna hear about what happened tonight," Ray-go said to me. "Even if they didn't do your dealers."

"I was thinking the same thing." Tony would use this as an excuse to continue his war with the Bloods. If he struck soon, it would appear to be payback.

"Tony's a master of neighborhood PR. He'll make this work for him." Ray-go's voice was full of admiration.

Ray-go reminded me of a young professor, and it wasn't just

because he wore glasses. He had a razor-sharp mind and took the game seriously. The other lieutenants looked up to him. If there was anyone to imitate, anyone who could show me how to walk the line, it was Ray-go. But I also knew that he was the one to watch out for. Of all the lieutenants, he was the most likely to sniff me out.

My phone buzzed in my pocket. It was a text from Busy.

@hospital. Doc says pfree got concushion + broken bones but will b ok.

P-Free would live after all. But someone else wouldn't. The war would continue. Diamond Tony would make sure of it.

HERE

The lieutenants stuck around until Chaos closed. I waited for Jessica to do whatever waitresses did at the end of the night, then she grabbed her coat and we left together. I held her close as we waited for a cab. Her hair smelled like liquor and cigars, but behind that was her natural scent. A few minutes before, I'd thought I was exhausted. Now my whole body was wide awake.

The cab dropped us at her building, and we went to our private place on the top floor. We curled up together on a couch.

Jessica yawned against my shoulder. "Let's stay here all night," she said, snuggling into me.

"Don't you have to go home?"

"I told my parents I was staying at Natalie's. I'd planned to . . . until you showed up."

"Sounds good to me. Don't forget you have class in the morning."

"So do you."

"I'm used to not getting much sleep. You're not."

"I've got first period free. And we're watching a movie in Randall's class. I can sleep."

"Okay. You comfortable?"

She smiled sleepily. "You're so caring. It's one of the things I love about you."

"Oh yeah? What are the other things?" This could be priceless. If I knew exactly what I was doing right, I'd be sure to keep doing it.

She lifted an eyebrow. "You want your ego stroked?"

"That ain't the only thing."

"Ha-ha. Seriously, though, you're a sweetheart. When I see you with Kiki, I can tell you'll be a good dad one day."

I smiled. I was glad she'd noticed that.

"You're really smart," she went on. "I don't mean school smart, though you're that, too, when you want to be. I mean smart like you see things for what they really are. You're not living in a dream world. And I don't want to sound superficial, but I love your muscles." She curled a hand around my biceps.

I tried not to pull away self-consciously. My arms had been

pretty good when I got out of juvie, but I needed to work out more to keep them that way. "I used to hate my chicken arms."

"You never had chicken arms. Not compared to the other guys, anyway. But you filled out."

"Thanks. Are you finished stroking my ego?" She could go on like this all night with no complaints from me.

"No, there's one more thing." She angled her face to look up at me. "I love your intensity, Darren. You're so determined. That's how I know you'll go places."

It was ironic, maybe. The same intensity that made her think I'd go places had also got me stuck in the game. Still, it felt good, real good, to hear her say those things. I'd wondered what she saw in me when she could have her pick of any guy.

We talked a little more, then faded into sleep. It felt great sleeping with Jessica in my arms, even if my neck was cranked the wrong way. She held me tight, despite being asleep. She held me like she thought I could disappear at any moment.

I didn't want to disappear. I didn't want to be anywhere but here.

REVELATION

When I got home the next morning, Tasha was on the couch watching TV. Usually she was in class by now.

She shot me a glare over her shoulder. "Oh, so you're finally making an appearance."

"Huh?"

"Staying out all night? Is that your thing now?"

I closed the door. "I was with Jessica. Is that a problem?"

"When I can't get in touch with you, it is." She stood up, ready for a fight. "Kiki's sick. I couldn't get through to you because you're not answering your phone. I missed my test."

"Oh." I would've said sorry, but it wasn't like I could've known. "How's Kiki?"

"He's sleeping. He's got a fever." Somehow she made it sound like that was my fault too.

"I'm here now." I glanced at my watch. "It's twenty to eight. You can still go."

"No point. My class starts at eight. It takes at least an hour to get there."

"I've got cash for a taxi."

"In rush-hour traffic? That would take even longer than the subway. Whatever." She crossed her arms and plunked back in front of the TV. "So I hear you're a lieutenant."

I was surprised—not that she knew, but that she'd brought it up. It was an unwritten code in our home that she and Mom never said a word about how I made money. After all, you can't criticize *and* lap up the cash.

"What I do is my business."

"If you get put away again, it's everybody's business."

"You sure you'll be able to afford to get your hair done if I quit? Because you and Mom never had a problem before."

"Don't lump me in with Mom. I've never used your money for my hair. *I* don't want you doing what you do. Mom, on the other hand, is hoping you'll become an executive so you can set her up nice."

Her words cut, because I knew they could be true. "Did she say that?"

"Didn't have to. I know Mom. Tell me, Darren. What kind of example are you setting for Kiki?"

"He doesn't know what I do. I'm not a lifetime player, anyway."

"Yeah, sure. You'd walk away from all that money."

"When the time is right, I will."

"If you're stupid enough to believe what you're saying, I bet you're using, too."

My patience was running out. "You're full of shit. Do I look like I'm using?"

"You sure look like our daddy."

I blinked. "What's that got to do with it?"

"Nothing." She turned up the TV.

I grabbed the remote and turned it off. "What are you talking about?"

"I'm staying out of this. It's between you and Mom."

I'd had enough of Tasha's games. "Tell me what you know or I'll break this remote over your skull."

She glanced at me nervously, not wanting to call my bluff. "Fine. Our dad was a drug addict."

"Yeah, right. They don't let you into the army if you're using."

"He was never in the army. He couldn't even hold down a job."

I felt like I'd been sucker punched. "Like you remember all this."

"I don't remember. Mom told me."

I shook my head. It didn't make any sense. "Why would she tell you and not me?"

"What, have you just met our mother? She thinks a boy needs a role model, so she made one up."

"So you're saying Dad's alive?" My mind was spinning.

"Nah. Mom said he turned up dead not long after he left us."

I couldn't believe it. Any of it. "But I have a picture of him in his uniform."

She shrugged. "That ain't Dad. I think it's some cousin. *Now* can I have the remote?"

I flung the remote across the room. It smashed against the wall.

A wail erupted from the bedroom. Tasha stood up and glared at me. "See what you did?"

"I got it." I stalked down the hall to the bedroom that Kiki shared with Mom. He was sitting in his tiny toddler bed, crying hard. When he saw me come in, he hiccupped before bursting into tears again.

Scooping him up, I hugged him tight against my chest. I wanted to cry too. I wanted to cry and scream, because I felt like a whole part of me had been ripped away. I felt like my dad had just died. It made me sick. I wanted to lash out against the pain. But instead I hugged my brother.

"Shhh . . . It's okay, little bro. It's okay. Shhhh." I felt his forehead. It was warm, but not burning hot.

Kiki's cries turned to soft whines, and after a while I laid him down and he went to sleep while I rubbed his back.

Life was going to be better for Kiki. I was going to make sure of it.

Illusions

The blood of a fiend
Is running through my veins
The dad I believed in
Was nothing but a shame
I thought I had the lineage
Of someone strong and pure
But the story's an illusion
The lies are like poison
No such thing as a hero
Nothing is for sure.

BURNED

arly Sunday morning I got a call from Kessler. She wanted
to meet ASAP.

Despite a late night with the lieutenants, I dragged
myself out of bed, showered, and headed for the subway. It was a
nice day for March, warm enough to break out Kiki's wagon and
pull him around the neighborhood. He was the only reason I was
still living at home, since I could hardly stand the sight of my mom.

I kept asking myself the same thing: What kind of mother
lied to her kid about his dad? The worst part was, I'd been stupid enough to believe her. She'd never had good answers to my
questions about my dad's military career. When I'd asked about his

pension, she'd said it was small because he hadn't been in the army very long. And I'd actually bought it. Looking back, she hadn't even been a good liar.

Now, whenever I saw a fiend on the street, I wondered if that's what my dad had been like. I'd believed he was a hero, but he was just another zombie.

I didn't say a word to Mom about what I knew. What would be the point? Nothing she could say would make it right.

As for Tasha, she took an evil satisfaction in my misery. "Poor baby boy," she'd always said, and now it hit me what that really meant. She hated that Mom had always tried to protect me. But it wasn't my fault she treated us differently. At least she'd told Tasha the truth.

I had to put it aside for now. There were more important things to deal with.

It took fifteen minutes to get to the Garden District address Kessler had given me. I walked up the steps of the brownstone and pulled open the heavy wooden door. The residents' names were listed behind a glass panel. Next to Apartment C, it said: Amber Kessler.

This was her place? I didn't think cops invited informants to their homes. But then, I wasn't an official CI anymore.

She buzzed me in.

Her apartment was one flight up, and she immediately ushered me in, locking the door behind me. It was small, probably a one-bedroom, cluttered with plants and books and magazines. The main room seemed to be a living room, dining room, and office all in one. I could picture Prescott coming in here, loosening his tie, and putting his feet up in front of the TV. The thought gave me a twinge. I missed the guy.

"I'll take your coat." Kessler hung it up. She wore sweats and sneakers, and her hair was in a messy ponytail. "I thought it was safest to meet here."

It made sense. If I hadn't met Prescott in public, the Vet would never have known about me.

"Nice crib you got."

"Thanks. Can I get you a drink? 7UP or orange juice?"

"I'm good."

We sat down across from each other.

"I assume Tony's responsible for the grenade attack," she said.

The grenade attack. It had happened two nights ago on the South Side. Someone had smashed a window of the Bloods' hangout and thrown a grenade inside. Four people had been burned, and two were in critical condition. The neighborhood was still reeling. Sure, everybody knew there'd be payback for what happened to Busy and P-Free. But the method was unusual. This was Toronto, not Afghanistan.

"Yeah, Tony's behind it. All of his people have been celebrating."

"Do you know who threw it or who was in the getaway car?"

I shook my head. "They keep the details quiet."

"Who would Tony use for a job like that?"

"He's got a few thugs working for him. But there are these two cousins, Tyrell and Remy. Everybody calls them the Cuz. I've seen a lot more of them since Pup got locked up. Could've been them." I didn't mention that they'd disposed of the Vet's body. She didn't need to know about that.

"Tell me more, Darren. Tell me everything about Tony's operation that you think could help me."

I told her what I knew. She wrote it all down on a pad of paper, interrupting only to clarify certain details.

"You could raid a stash house easy," I said. "There'd be an exec there, maybe a lieutenant or two, and lots of cash and product. But I know these guys, and they won't talk. You wouldn't find anything that would point to Tony. He hardly ever shows up at the stash houses, and when he does, it's for five minutes, tops."

"That's our problem. He gives orders but never gets his hands dirty." She put down her pad. "You've been really helpful to me."

Interesting that she said "me" instead of "us," like Prescott used to. Since the cops had decided to charge Andre with Prescott's murder despite Kessler's warnings, I guess she was on her own now.

"Not helpful enough. I'm not getting us where we need to be."

"I'm going to put Tony away," she said. "That isn't going to change. But I don't want you taking this kind of risk. It's all or nothing for you, Darren. If Tony finds out, you're dead."

"I know that. You don't have to try to talk me out of this. It won't work. I'm going to see it through."

"You're determined, all right," she said. "But if you change your mind, it's never too late to get out."

"I hear you."

She picked up her pad again. "I'm going to look into a few neighborhood businesses. I'm hoping to find some connection to Walker or one of his executives. Any idea where I should start?"

"Look into a club called Chaos," I said. "Tony and his executives hang out there all the time. I wouldn't be surprised if he was laundering money through the place. But I bet you won't find his name on paper. He's too careful to put his name on anything that could burn him."

"He'll slip up sooner or later. Everyone does. No operation is airtight."

She was right. Tony would slip up, and I'd be there when he did.

"I'm counting on it."

CHAOS

Friday night, I went to Chaos with the crew. I was in a good mood because it was spring break next week. Without school in the way, Jessica and I could spend a lot more time together.

Diamond Tony and his execs were chilling in the VIP corner with a bunch of girls. Tony was known for being a lady's man. Rumor had it he never got with the same girl twice. I could never tell if his girls were paid, or if they just wanted a chance to get with a legend, like groupies with rock stars.

"You're happy tonight," Ray-go said. He was way too perceptive, but I probably wasn't hard to read. Jessica and I were going to sleep in the rec room tonight. We'd even hidden an air mattress and blankets up there so we'd be real cozy.

"I'm off school next week."

"Oh yeah, I forgot you still went." Ray-go chuckled. He knew I still lived at home. He probably thought I was going to school because my mom made me. "So what do you want to be when you grow up?"

"Rich."

"You're in the right biz for that." We bumped fists.

As the lieutenants talked, drank, and surveyed the girls on the dance floor, I kept searching for glimpses of Jessica. Every time I saw her, I felt my blood race. I still couldn't believe she was mine.

Ray-go nudged me. "Check out that guy with the red hair. What's he been smoking?"

It was Cam. He was dancing his heart out behind a gorgeous girl, doing the running man, the robot, the horse-riding dance, anything to make his friends crack up. Whenever the girl turned around, he ignored her and pretended to dance with his friends.

"That's my man Cam. He's class all the way."

We watched and laughed, but seeing Cam fazed me. Memories flashed before my eyes—the Vet lying dead, Cam freaking out, the Cuz packaging the body like a carcass of meat. I took a long swig of beer, followed by another, wishing the alcohol could erase it all from my mind.

A few minutes later, I headed to the bathroom, and on my way out, I ran into Cam. I had the feeling he'd been waiting there for me.

"Kudos on the promo," Cam said, but I didn't buy the smile. In fact, his congrats sounded more like a condolence.

"Yeah, that's me. How's everything going on our old corner? Wallop treating you good?"

"You didn't hear? I got out. Couple weeks ago." He shuffled his feet. "It was time to retire, you know?"

"I know." I wasn't going to say it, but I was glad for him. "Good luck with your GED."

I gave him a one-armed hug. For a second, his grip tightened. "Get out, Dare. It ain't worth it."

That's when I knew: Cam had believed the Vet. He knew I was a snitch. But instead of selling me out, he had my back.

"Thanks, man."

There was nothing for me to do but walk away. I'd gotten the message loud and clear. But I was in too deep. And Cam probably knew that.

Back at my table, I finished my beer, which had gone flat, and pretended to listen to one of the lieutenants' stories about his crazy ex-girlfriend. Cam's warning didn't change anything. I knew the danger, but I couldn't dwell on it. As an informant, I had to lock away my fear. It was the only way I could keep going.

When last call came, we settled our bill. The total for our table was always over five hundred, sometimes more than a thousand. If Tony was behind this place, it would work out pretty sweet for him. His employees spent a shitload of their money here, which put it right back into his pocket.

The lieutenants headed out, and I waited by the bar for Jessica to get ready. Tony and his entourage lingered at their table. Last call meant nothing to them. Nobody would dare ask them to leave.

Lucky for me, Jessica wasn't serving their tables, so she was done for the night. I put my arm around her as we walked out.

"Oh! I forgot to pick up my check. I'll just be a minute." She hurried back inside. I waited, talking with the doorman, a hulk called Rashid. He used to work for Tony years ago but had taken several bullets in the leg and now walked with a cane. I'd seen him use that cane to beat the snot out of anyone who messed with him.

Diamond Tony and his executives came out with their girls. I guess they'd decided to move the party to a more intimate location. Vinny slapped my back. He was obviously drunk but happy as hell. He'd been on cloud nine since he'd become an executive. And why shouldn't he be? He had everything he'd ever wanted—money, girls, status. He was living the dream.

"Darren, my man," he said, like we were best friends. "I hear you got your corners locked down."

"You taught me all I know."

He grinned at that, and I noticed another gold tooth in his smile. "Always said you was a good soljah." He turned to Jessica, who'd come out of the club. "Hey, Jessica." He looked her up and down, his grin broadening.

I put an arm around her protectively.

Diamond Tony walked up behind Vinny and clapped a hand on his shoulder. "Respect a man's property now."

Vinny laughed. "Always do."

"Darren," Tony said with a nod. "Jessica." He smiled at her, and I fought to control my reaction. Of course he knew her, I told myself. She'd probably waited on him many times.

"I have cars coming if you'd like a ride," Tony said, directing the question to me.

"Thanks, but we'll get a—"

Gunshots. Jessica and I hit the pavement. I crouched over her, sheltering her with my body.

People ran for cover or dove to the ground. Diamond Tony sprinted behind a parked car, firing his semiautomatic. One of his execs, Kamal, was facedown on the sidewalk. All I could do was stay low and protect Jessica.

Tires screeched and the car sped away. Tony fired several shots after it, then gave up.

Gradually people started coming out in the open—Tony's guys, clubbers, bystanders. Tony was bent over Kamal, swearing. Rashid was giving someone chest compressions. Vinny was still huddled beside us on the ground.

I touched Jessica's back. "It's okay, they're gone. Let's get out of here before the cops come."

She didn't answer. Sirens reached a fever pitch as emergency crews got closer to the scene.

"Jessica?" Panic cut through me. "Jessica, talk to me!"

I turned her onto her back. Her chest was soaked with blood.

CORRIDOR

I held Jessica's hand all the way to the hospital, then she was torn away from me and rushed to the operating room.

I called her parents, told them Jessica had been shot and that she was at North York General.

If she dies, I'll die. If she dies, I'll die.

In the men's room, I broke down.

Don't die. Please don't die.

I stumbled out of the bathroom, stopping a nurse, asking her to find out what was happening to my girlfriend. She ushered me to the waiting room and told me that someone would come back and tell me.

No one came. I sat there for minutes that felt like hours. I stared down the long corridor at the automatic doors they'd taken her through.

It wasn't long before Jessica's family arrived. They were sleep rumpled, and Kendra was still in pajamas. They spoke to a nurse at reception.

I knew I should go up to them, say something. It was the last thing I wanted to do. If I talked to them, they'd see my guilt. They'd know this was my fault.

I forced myself to go over. The moment Jessica's mom saw me, she grabbed my arm. "You were with her, Darren. You saw what happened?"

"I met her after work," I said, leading Mrs. Thomas to the waiting area. We sat down. "We were waiting outside the club for a cab, talking to some people. And then the shooting started. It came from a car. I never even saw it pull up."

"They just started shooting people?" her dad asked. "Were they after someone?"

"A lot of dealers hang out there. They must've been the targets."

I felt Kendra's eyes on me. She knew that I was one of those dealers. If she was going to tell her parents, that was up to her. Part of me wanted her to—that way they'd hate me as much as I hated myself right now.

"Was Diamond Tony there?" Kendra asked. Her eyes were red from crying. There was no blame in them, just grief.

I nodded. "He might've been the one they were after."

Jessica's dad was bewildered. "Who's Diamond Tony?"

"Big drug dealer," Kendra said.

"We never should've let her work there." Jessica's mom turned to her husband. "Did you know drug dealers went there?"

"Of course not. She said it was an upscale place."

"It is a nice place, Mrs. Thomas," I said, trying to reassure her. "I haven't heard of any trouble there before."

We sat in silence for a while. Every time the doors opened, we hoped someone would give us an update on Jessica. But no one came. The waiting room got so crowded with people waiting for news on the gunshot victims that I gave up my seat. I was sick of sitting still anyway.

I paced the hallways. At one point a doctor came out and spoke to a woman in a hijab. Her son, Kamal, was dead.

Minutes later, another doctor, another family. Pox was dead too.

Two executives dead. Several people wounded. Jessica fighting for her life.

And Diamond Tony had walked away.

A pair of cops showed up and started questioning anyone who

was present at the shooting. Eventually they came to me. I spoke to them briefly in the hallway, out of earshot from Jessica's family.

I didn't know these cops, and they didn't know me. To them, I was a bystander who'd been in the wrong place at the wrong time with his girlfriend. They didn't know I had been Prescott's CI, and I wasn't going to tell them. Since I wasn't a suspect, there was no point in complicating things. I told them that I lived in the area and that there seemed to be a turf war going on between rival gangs. No, I hadn't gotten a good look at the shooters or their car. I wished I had.

They accepted my answers. There was no reason not to. It wasn't like anyone here was going to tell them I was a dealer. And I'd put money on no one mentioning Diamond Tony or the Bloods. They all knew the code.

The cops moved on to question someone else, and I went back to Jessica's family. We waited for at least another hour.

Finally, an update.

An Asian doctor in scrubs came through the doors and stood in the middle of the waiting area. "Jessica Thomas's family?"

We stood up and rushed toward him.

"Your daughter made it through the initial surgery," he told her parents. "We've managed to extract the bullet from her chest cavity. Because of the amount of blood loss, we've given her several transfusions. Right now we have her in an induced coma. It will give her body a chance to recover."

"Is she going to be okay?" Kendra asked.

"Her condition is still critical. We'll have a better idea in the next few days."

JUSTICE

The following night Vinny found me in the waiting room.

"I hear she pulled through surgery." He sat down beside me. "That's good."

I didn't say anything.

"You been here this whole time?" he asked.

I nodded.

"I don't want you to worry about your corners. They're being looked after. Tony wanted me to check on you. Make sure you're okay."

"What do *you* think?"

Vinny didn't try to answer that. "Let me know if there's anything I can do."

"There is. Tell Tony that bullet should've been *his*."

I didn't care about the consequences. What I said was true and Vinny knew it. That bullet was meant for Tony, but Jessica had taken the hit. For what?

"We lost two execs, you know. Kamal and Pox. Tony's pretty broken up about it."

"I'm sure he is." With half of his executives gone, Tony would have to step up, at least until he could replace them. He couldn't stay in the shadows the way he liked to.

Vinny went stone serious. "Tony wanted me to give you a message."

"Oh yeah?" There was nothing Tony could say that I wanted to hear.

"The people who did this are gonna face justice. Diamond style."

RECKONING

Two days ticked by. I prayed to God. I wasn't sure if I believed, but Jessica did. So if there was a God, I bet he'd be there for her.

Jessica was in an induced coma so she wouldn't fight the ventilator. Everything I heard the doctors and nurses say scared the hell out of me—they talked about blood loss and tissue damage, fractured ribs, a collapsed lung. But she was hanging on. She had to hang on.

Her family and I were in and out of the ICU day and night. Her parents requested that I be able to see her even though I wasn't immediate family. I guess they thought Jessica would want me there.

At some point Tasha and Mom showed up. Mom said things like, "Don't worry, honey, she'll be okay," and "She's a strong girl, she'll pull through." Like my mom could know. Her words were the same as always: empty. As for Tasha, she didn't make any false promises, she just said, "I'm here for you." Yeah, right. It took balls for her to come here and offer me support. I didn't need either of them, and I told them so.

Vinny left several messages on my voice mail. When I didn't return his calls, he left another message saying they were replacing me until I was ready to come back.

Was I going back?

I had no idea. Part of me wanted to stay in the game. I wasn't afraid for my life anymore. My life didn't mean shit when Jessica was fighting for hers.

But Jessica had wanted me out of Tony's business more than anything. And if this was my chance to get out without Diamond Tony being suspicious, maybe I should take it.

The Price

The cost of war can't be measured
In dollars or in cents
Why do the good ones

219

Always have to pay the rent
For crimes they don't commit
For things they haven't done
When bullets start flying
There's nowhere to run.

THE VISITOR

I woke up to find White Chris in the chair beside me, eating a bag of chips. I didn't know what time of day it was.

"How did you . . . ?" I rubbed my eyes. I couldn't remember if I'd called him or not.

"Tasha messaged me on Facebook. She told me what happened. Said you could use some support."

That was Tasha—always sticking her nose in. But I had to admit, it was good to see White Chris. I should've contacted him myself.

"Thought you might be hungry." He handed me a bag of chips and a bottle of Pepsi.

"Thanks." I couldn't remember the last time I'd eaten anything. I shoved some chips into my mouth.

He looked at me with his good eye. "How is she?"

"There are all these complications. They want to keep her in a coma." Even as I said it, it didn't feel real.

"How are you holding up?"

"When I know she's okay, I'll be okay. That's all."

"Take care of yourself, Darren. The last thing she needs to wake up to is a smelly boyfriend."

I raised my eyebrows. "I stink?"

"Let's put it this way: Eau Sauvage doesn't smell better on the third day. Now eat your chips. She wouldn't want you getting scrawny, either."

"You're harsh."

I finished the bag of chips, then washed them down with the Pepsi. We sat in silence for a while. With the food and drink in my system, my mind felt clearer. But it only made the guilt worse.

"I'm the reason she's in there, Chris. Me. I shouldn't have been standing with her outside the club. Not when there's a turf war going on. It was stupid."

"Jessica works at Chaos. She would've been there with or without you. Torturing yourself won't help her."

"I can't help her. That's the problem."

"Actually, you can. She's going to pull through this part. And when she wakes up, she's going to need you. Remember when I was laid up with a smashed eye, and instead of playing violins, you were bitching at me to finish the songs we were working on?"

A reluctant smile pulled at my mouth. "What was I supposed to do? You were using the eye thing as an excuse not to write."

"I was so jacked on pain meds, none of my lyrics made sense. But you made me keep at it anyway."

"Damn right. Remember when your aunt told you that girls loved eye patches because it reminded them of Johnny Depp?"

White Chris chuckled. "You said that was the biggest pile of bullshit you ever heard. And that my only prayer of getting a girl was becoming a rich music producer."

"It's still true."

"Point is, you helped me out." He paused, shaking his head. "And I had no clue you were plotting revenge against Jongo the whole time."

"It had to be done."

White Chris glanced at me warily, as if he was wondering if I had another scheme up my sleeve. "It's over, right? This whole thing?"

That was one question I couldn't answer.

IN

More days passed. I didn't know how many. And then I got a text from Vinny that I couldn't ignore.

DT wants 2 C U. 24 Wind Terrace.

It was decision time.

I knew I had to move quickly or Diamond Tony would be gone when I got there. He never stayed long in meeting locations.

Within half an hour, I showed up at the address on the northeast side. I'd been here before. It was the boarded-up town house with the cushy living room where I thought I'd be murdered but instead was promoted to lieutenant. I went up the steps and was met by the Cuz.

"Don't take it personal, but we gotta pat you down," Tyrell said.

"We do it to everybody these days," Remy added. "Tony's orders."

I spread my arms and legs for the pat down.

Then I stepped inside. I walked down the dingy hall into the living room. Tony and Vinny were waiting.

"Darren, my man." Tony came up to me, grabbing my hand and giving me a back pound. "How's Jessica?"

The sound of her name on his lips made me sick. I wanted to kill him right then and there. "Alive."

"Good. Vinny gave me your message."

I didn't give a fuck if I'd pissed him off. I'd meant every word. That bullet should've hit him instead of Jessica.

"You were right," Tony said evenly. "That bullet was meant for me. And your girl took it. I respect your sacrifice."

I stared at him blankly. He made it sound like Jessica took the bullet to save his life. He was totally deluded.

"I know this has been a hard time for you, Darren. Has been for all of us. You heard about Kamal and Pox."

"Yeah."

"In times like these, we have to stick together. You feel me?"

Now would be the time to tell him I was done. I wanted out. But before I could say anything, he spoke again. "I've lost good soldiers, Darren. But I have a business to run. I need to promote two lieutenants to executive positions. Ray-go has agreed to step up. And both he and Vinny recommended you."

It took a second for his words to register.

I wasn't sure what to say. I needed to think, but I couldn't think with Tony watching me.

"I know you're wondering why I haven't dealt with the Bloods who did this yet. I promise you, I will. Our revenge will be brutal and complete. It will be a Blood bath." He smiled.

My gut twisted.

"I need a decision from you, Darren. Being an executive is a privilege. Vinny can tell you all about it. But you've got to devote yourself to it. I need to know you'll be on your game even though your girl's in the hospital."

When I hesitated, he went on. "If you become an executive, you can be a part of the retaliation against the Bloods."

My mind spun. If I turned down the position, I'd be giving up my best chance to put him away. I'd be giving up my chance to avenge Jessica, Prescott, and everyone else Tony had hurt or killed.

It was now or never.

A smile came to my lips. "I'm in."

DREAMLAND

I stood next to Jessica's bed, holding her hand. She'd always been beautiful when she slept, and she still was, even hooked up to those machines. Her face looked peaceful, but I knew that inside her, it was a different story. She was fighting to come back, I could feel it.

I tried to think of something to say. "You should see Kiki these days. He's all about his keyboard. He knows which buttons to press for which beats. He tries to do some beat boxing, but he just ends up spitting everywhere. It's so cute. I've got a video on my phone. I'll show you when you wake up."

Her lips twitched, unless I was imagining it. She always reacted when I mentioned Kiki. Part of me wished I could bring him in here, to see if she'd react to his voice. But Kiki wasn't allowed in the ICU, and it was probably best. He'd get upset if he saw her this way. And I wouldn't want Jessica to hear him cry.

Tears burned my eyes.

"I'm sorry, Jessica. Sorry I got you involved in all this. I'm gonna make things right. No matter what, I'll make things right."

I squeezed her hand. I couldn't be sure, but she might have squeezed mine back.

THE NEW GENERATION

To the new execs!" Vinny lifted his champagne flute.

Ray-go and I clinked glasses with the others. We'd been executives for all of two days, and the party had never stopped. These guys played hard. I wasn't sure if they worked hard too.

I sipped my champagne. It was the expensive stuff, but I could hardly tell. Vinny was bragging about how he got with three girls in one night, and everybody was loving the story. Even the girl sitting on his lap seemed to enjoy it. Maybe she'd been one of them.

We were at the Rockefeller, an upscale lounge downtown. The doormen had ushered us in like celebrities.

"Congrats, Darren," said the girl to my right. She was just like all the others who hung around Tony and the execs—sexy and eager as hell to be someone's girl. Judging by the way Ray-go and I had been pawed over the past couple of days, we were fresh meat.

"How does it feel being big-time?" she asked, batting her fake eyelashes.

"Good." I took a sip of champagne.

She didn't recognize me, but I recognized her. Tamara Knox had been a senior when I was a freshman. I bet every guy in the school had fantasized about her. She reminded me of Nicki Minaj with her pink wig, big bootie, and annoying voice.

"Let's dance," Tamara said, taking my hand and massaging her thumb in my palm.

Why not? My face hurt from smiling at their stupid stories. I needed a break.

I could hear the other girls snickering as Tamara led me away. The dance floor was packed with couples juggling drinks and dancing sexy. Tamara's arms snaked around my neck. "I didn't tell you my name, did I? I'm Jayda."

I knew she wasn't, but I didn't care. She could be whoever she wanted.

"You move nice," she said.

Actually, I was hardly moving at all. "You too."

She flattened her body against mine and grinned like a cat. "This is nothing. You should see what else I can do."

I felt a shot of anger. She must've known my girl was lying in a hospital bed. But she saw this as her chance to get with one of the new execs.

Vinny came onto the floor with two girls. They seemed happy to sandwich him between them. He nudged me with his elbow and shouted over the music, "Don't get better than this!"

But it *did* get worse. How long did Vinny think he could stay on top?

Speaking of on top, Tamara—Jayda—was all over me. It was time to cut her loose. I told her I had to go to the bathroom and I'd meet her back at the table. When I returned, I sat by Ray-go instead. She looked mad enough to spit.

I poured myself another drink, just for something to do, and said to Ray-go, "I thought being a lieutenant was it. But being an exec, man, this is ridiculous."

"I know. It's like every door is open. Nothing's off-limits. This is how it should be."

I studied him. "You always knew you'd get here one day, didn't you?"

"Yeah, but not this soon. You?"

"No way. I got lucky."

"Some things are meant to be. And if we play our cards right, we're here to stay." He took a sip of champagne. "Don't forget, the kingpin's going to pass on his crown one day. And you and me, we're the new generation."

EXECUTIVE DECISION

t was my first executive meeting.

Mom would be proud.

We sat around a polished table in a swanky crib—whose crib, I didn't know. The room was long and rectangular with dark hardwood floors and real artwork on the walls. It felt like a cross between an upscale boardroom and a classy dining room. We drank whiskey as we waited for Diamond Tony to start the meeting.

I'd learned more in my first few days as an executive than in months of street dealing. Tony's executives were no different than the executives of a Fortune 500 company. We were the leaders of the organization, the advisers to the CEO. All the dirty jobs went to the underlings. The closest an executive ever got to the street was when he took his turn running the stash house. Otherwise, it was white collar all the way.

So far, my main job was to drop off cash at businesses that laundered money for Tony. Vinny came with me. We stopped by a beauty shop, a pawnshop, a deli, a bakery, and Chaos—no surprise there.

Problem was, I didn't see Tony's name on anything. Every transaction was in cash and every agreement was verbal. Tony had no formal ties to the business owners. I bet he hadn't even met most of them.

"It's time," Diamond Tony said.

Everybody hushed. His mood was intense today. I was pretty sure I knew what the meeting was about.

"We've had a lot of business to lock down these days, but everybody did their part. Even our newbies." He nodded toward Ray-go and me. "I want to catch you up on the plan for dealing with the Bloods."

Marcus took it from there. "We've got a snitch in the Bloods. He's going to tell us the location of their next meeting. Then our guys will go in with guns blazing."

Ray-go frowned. "That could be a while, right? I doubt they'll be getting together this soon after the shootings. They'll be lying low."

"Lately they've been meeting in busy public places—bars, restaurants," Marcus said. "They feel safe there."

Tony snorted. "They ain't."

My gut tightened. Tony was going to shoot up a public place. Taking revenge on the Bloods responsible for the drive-by was one thing, but catching innocent people in the crossfire was another. I couldn't let that happen.

"We've got floor plans of their main hangouts," Marcus told us. "All we need is half an hour's notice, and our guys are good to go."

Damn. If it was a last-minute thing, how would I ever stop it?

There was only one option I could think of.

"I want to . . ." My voice sounded weak, so I cleared my throat. "I want to be there."

Tony shook his head. "I want to keep my execs' hands clean. No unnecessary risks." He turned back to Marcus as if the conversation was over.

I didn't let it go. "Those fuckers shot my girl in cold blood. I want to be there. I want to pull the trigger myself."

"You used a semiauto before?" Tony asked.

"No."

He smiled. "It don't matter. It's mad easy." He pretended to pull a trigger with his index finger. "You just squeeze and—pop, pop, pop!"

The execs laughed.

"Okay, Darren," Tony said. "I respect that you want to do the job yourself." There was a glint of admiration in his eyes. "Fact is, I'm the same way."

AWAKENING

When Jessica woke up, I was there, holding her hand.

At first, her eyes seemed lost, searching for something. But then they found a point to focus on: me.

"Jessica." I touched her cheek. "I missed you so much."

She was looking right at me, but her expression didn't change. It was like she was in a different world. That was the medication, I reminded myself. They were keeping her heavily sedated so she wouldn't be in pain.

"It'll be okay, I promise. I know you can't talk because of the ventilator, but you'll be able to soon. We have to be patient." I patted her hand. "Can you feel that?"

She blinked. I wondered if that meant something.

"Just sit tight. Everyone says you're doing great."

She didn't respond. I had no idea if she could hear me.

I leaned forward and kissed her cheek. "I love you, Jessica."

Her eyes closed.

GUN RUN

It was Vinny who took me to get a gun. He seemed excited, like he was showing his little brother how to play ball for the first time.

"Our guys usually get their guns off the streets," he explained in the car. "Not us execs. We go to the best place in town. Most gangstas live their whole lives in this city and don't even know this guy exists."

"This guy" was called Gallinger. We met him at his hardware store in North York. He had big shoulders, graying blond hair, and little round glasses. He wore a checkered shirt and jeans under a red apron.

The only other employee in the store looked like a younger version of Gallinger, maybe his son. He glanced at us for a second, then went back to showing a customer some paint samples.

Gallinger's real business was two floors below the hardware store, down a maze of concrete halls. He stopped in front of a massive steel door, which he opened using a key card. We found ourselves in a huge gray room full of guns. Long guns of every description were mounted on the walls, while handguns were in glass cases. They were perfectly displayed and labeled, like exhibits in a museum.

I looked around in awe. "How'd you get all this in here?" I asked.

Gallinger scowled at Vinny, who said to him quickly, "Don't pay him no mind."

The old guy wasn't impressed. "What do we want?"

Vinny started talking in gun lingo. Brand names, numbers, rpm. I caught the words "easy" and "semiautomatic."

I was going to have a gun. It was just for show, of course, since Kessler and I had a plan to stop the massacre, but I still didn't like it. All I knew was, our plan had better work or a lot of people would die.

I snapped awake as a silver gun was handed to me. I tested the weight. It felt heavy, cold.

"Easy. Fast. Guaranteed to never jam," Gallinger said.

"How does it feel?" Vinny asked me.

"Powerful."

Vinny smiled, flashing his gold teeth. "We'll take it."

I reached for my wallet, but Vinny shook his head. "Trust me, you ain't got enough cash in there to pay for a weapon like this." He said to Gallinger, "Tony's account."

Gallinger nodded.

"We need ammo, too," Vinny added, giving me a wink. "Lots of it."

BLOOD BATH

The call finally came at eleven thirty Saturday night.

"Late show. Fifteen minutes. Wait outside." Marcus hung up.

I called Kessler. "They're picking me up in fifteen minutes. I've got the cell on me. You're sure you can track it with the GPS?"

"We're on it. And, Darren, if things go wrong, get out of there."

"I hear you."

Since I was already dressed, there was nothing to do but leave. And take the gun with me.

It wasn't long before an old Chevy pulled up. When I got in, the guys were pumped up, and so was the radio. As I'd suspected, the Cuz were in the car. The driver was Ashtray, a member of Tony's security entourage.

"How close are we?" I asked above the music.

"Seven minutes, maybe," Tyrell shouted from the passenger seat. "You ready? I heard you ain't popped nobody before."

"One of those motherfuckers shot my girlfriend. My finger ain't gonna shake on the trigger."

"Amen to that!" Ashtray said.

The Cuz were high. I could tell from their wild eyes, the way they bounced in their seats. I wasn't surprised. Diamond Dust made a man feel invincible and gave him permission to do vicious things.

As the night flashed by the window, I kept waiting for a police car to stop us. I wasn't sure if it would be a marked or unmarked car.

With every second that passed, I got more nervous.

What if the cops didn't come through? What would I do then?

"Two minutes, boys," said Ashtray, pressing pedal to metal.

Two minutes. My internal panic button switched on. *Where the fuck are the cops?*

"Two minutes till showtime!" Tyrell pulled out a sleek silver gun. It was a nice piece, sophisticated like mine. Probably from Gallinger's. Something clicked in my brain.

"Sweet semiauto," I shouted over the front seat.

Tyrell threw a worried look over his shoulder. "Don't go telling you-know-who about it, 'kay? I'm not supposed to still have it."

"Yo, slow up a bit, Ash!" Remy shouted from next to me. "We don't want to get stopped."

"A'ight, a'ight. How about this?" Ashtray came to a full stop at the next stop sign. "Y'all ready? It's that building half a block—"

A siren wailed as an unmarked cop car drove up behind us.

"What the fuck?" Tyrell called out.

"Oh shit." Ashtray started up slow, like he was taking his driver's test. "Do I pull over?"

"Go go go!" Tyrell barked. "They find these guns and we're fucked!"

Ashtray slammed on the brakes, causing the cop cruiser to rear-end us. Then he floored the gas. The tires screeched as he plowed forward, taking a right and blasting down the street.

I grabbed on to the seat in front of me as we took another corner. We lost the cops quickly, but Ashtray drove around for another few minutes to make sure. Eventually, he pulled to a stop in the lot where Diamond Tony kept his extra cars.

I breathed a sigh of relief. The tracker on my cell had worked. The Blood bath had been stopped.

For now.

POST MORTEM

An hour later, we were at the stash house with Diamond Tony, Marcus, and Vinny.

I'd never seen Tony so pissed. He looked at Ashtray. "How the fuck did you get pulled over half a block from the club?"

Ashtray shrank back. "I dunno. Just a bad coincidence."

"Fuck coincidences." Tony advanced on him. Ashtray was tall and stocky, but when Tony got close, he cowered. "You hear me? I don't believe in coincidences."

We had our backs to the wall like we were waiting for a firing squad. "Why did you get pulled over?" Tony's eyes landed on me. "Darren?"

"It's hard to tell. Cops are everywhere these days. Everybody's getting stopped."

His nostrils flared. "Come over here, Darren. You're an exec." I went over to stand with Marcus and Vinny. What a relief. He turned on Ashtray again. "You were speeding, weren't you?"

"Not much. I mean, I was driving normal. Going the speed limit makes us way more suspicious. But Remy told me to slow up."

Tony got in Remy's face. "You told him to slow up?"

"Yeah. I didn't wanna get stopped."

"It ain't about me going too fast or too slow," Ashtray said. "Darren's right—everybody's getting stopped for no reason."

Tony's hands were clenched at his sides. "I don't like fuckups. We'll try again another time. And if it don't go down like I think it should, somebody's gonna pay. You hear me?"

They all nodded.

"Now get out of my sight." He waved a hand and they bolted out of there. "All they had to do was go in there and pull the trigger. Fuck!"

We said nothing, just watched him as he paced. When he stopped, he focused on Marcus. "Maybe we should do it ourselves. I need to know these Bloods are gonna taste bullets."

Marcus shook his head. "Too big and messy a job, Tony."

He paced some more. "You're right."

"Fuckups happen," Marcus assured him. "You know the Cuz will come through."

Tony's eyes settled on me. "We'll get this thing done, Darren. For your girl. For my execs. We'll get it done. But next time, I don't want you involved." When he saw that I was about to argue, he put up his hand. "If you'd been pulled over, you could be sitting on weapons charges right now. I ain't risking another exec."

I was silent.

"What do y'all think about Remy?" he asked. "Think he's loyal? See, what I just heard was that he told Ashtray to slow the car just before the cops showed up. That right, Darren?"

"Guess so."

"That's some timing, don't you think?"

"You think he's snitching?" Vinny asked.

"Maybe. I don't trust anyone but my execs."

With any luck, that would be Tony's downfall.

THE PLAY

The next night, I went to Kessler's apartment.

"Darren." She'd been expecting me and waved me in quickly. She must have just gotten back from work, since she was still wearing office clothes and an ID badge. Judging from the bags under her eyes, she was worn out.

"You did well last night," she said. "Did Walker suspect anything?"

"He has some suspicions about one of the guys, but I don't think it'll come to anything. We convinced him it was a random stop."

"Good."

We sat down.

"I'm sure they'll try again soon," she said.

"They will, unless we can throw them off."

"What do you have in mind?"

"I think I know where the gun is that killed Prescott."

She gasped. "You do?"

"Tyrell has it. He's one of the Cuz, those cousins who do dirty jobs for Tony. He was planning to use it for the attack on the Bloods. He told me not to tell Tony that he still had it. It's got to be the murder weapon."

"I'll get a search warrant for Tyrell's place. We'll find that gun."

I hated to dampen her hope, but I said, "Even if you find it, I don't think Tyrell's gonna rat on Tony. He's a thug through and through."

"When he's given a choice between life without parole and a reduced sentence, he'll choose what's good for him."

I shook my head. "You don't know this guy. He'll be afraid that if he gives up Tony, he'll be dead before he has a chance to testify. How are you gonna keep him safe in prison? And what about his family on the outside?"

She thought about it. "We'll offer all the protection we can. It's a cop-killer case, so that'll give us leverage. I can get some security for his family, at least for a couple of weeks. I'll keep his cousin Remy out of the mix entirely, if that's what it takes. I could get Tyrell transferred out of town, somewhere beyond Tony's reach. It's more than the scumbag deserves, but Ed would want Tony put away."

She was right about that.

OFF-LIMITS

When I first saw Jessica smile, I knew she was back. The light was in her eyes again.

Within twenty-four hours she was off the ventilator and able to talk.

"The nurse says you're doing amazing," I told her. It was early evening, a week after my debriefing with Kessler, and I had some spare time before I had to go back to the stash house. "I bet you're the strongest patient they've ever seen."

"That's me." Her voice was still shaky. "A medical miracle."

"Seriously, you should give yourself some credit. You bounced back fast."

"Not fast enough for me." Her face looked tight, and I knew she was in pain. I offered her the pump for more drugs, but she didn't take it. "I'm fine. I want to stay awake. Did you ask about the TV? Every channel is fuzzy."

Jessica hated to get behind on her favorite shows. It was a good sign. "The lady at the desk took care of it. It should be working already. Want to watch something?"

"It's okay. It's just for when I'm alone."

When I'm alone. I knew she didn't mean anything by it, but it made me wish that I could be with her more. I hated that I'd let her down so much in the past, and now, when she really needed me, where was I? Working for Tony. No way I'd tell her that I'd become an executive.

At that moment my phone buzzed. I glanced down, relieved to see that it was only Tasha. I ignored the call.

"Somebody's edgy," Jessica said. She was still perceptive, despite all the meds. "Everything okay?"

"Yeah, everything's cool. It was just Tasha."

"Oh." She wasn't Tasha's biggest fan either. "When am I gonna see Kiki? I miss him."

"Soon." Guilt washed over me. Now that she was out of ICU and off the ventilator, I should've brought Kiki in to visit her. But with all my responsibilities as an executive, I hadn't had the chance.

"How's school? Everybody still asking about me?"

I had to smile. "No one talks about anything else." Truth was, I'd hardly been at school since the shooting, but I didn't want her to know that.

The door opened, and Jessica's mom walked in. She looked so small and frail as she approached Jessica's bed and took her hand. At least now that Jessica was awake, she wasn't crying all the time.

I kissed Jessica and left the room. Since I wasn't due back at the stash house yet, I figured I'd stop in at home to see if I'd heard from Kessler. I hadn't checked the secret cell since lunchtime, and I hoped Kessler had gotten the warrant for Tyrell's apartment by now.

If I was lucky, I'd also catch Kiki before bed.

I drove home in the Lexus that Marcus had rented for me. I'd have preferred a car that didn't attract so much attention, especially because rumor had it the Bloods were itching to take out more of Tony's team. But driving some beater car wasn't an option. The ride was part of the executive mystique.

When I got in the door, Mom and Tasha were watching TV. Kiki must've already gone to bed.

I went to my room and grabbed the phone from under my mattress.

No messages.

How long could it possibly take for a judge to sign a piece of paper? Kessler had to get that gun from Tyrell before he got rid of it. I was counting on the fact that he wanted it for the Blood bath and would keep it until that was over. But he could wise up and dump it at any time. I wished I hadn't commented on it in the car—I was an executive, and that might've spooked him. He could worry I'd tell Tony.

"How many phones do you have, anyway?" Tasha asked, leaning in the doorway. Just like her to sneak in without knocking.

"Mind your business."

"Did you see that I called you?"

"Oh yeah. You did. Checking up on baby boy?"

"Kiki wanted to know when you were coming home. He misses you." She crossed her arms. "I've been wondering something."

"What's that?"

"Why you haven't moved out yet. You're an exec now, right? You must be swimming in green."

She was at it again. I forced myself to stay cool. "I'm staying here because of Kiki. I know I haven't been around much lately, but that'll change soon. I don't need to explain myself to you. You're not the one paying the rent. If Mom wants me out, I'll get out."

"Mom wants *you* to pay the rent, that's what she wants. Anyway, I was thinking we should make up a story for Kiki about what his brother does. Because I don't think a drug dealer—no, sorry, an executive to the kingpin—is much of a role model."

"Kiki's a good judge of character. See whose arms he runs to next time we're both in the room."

"Can't argue with that. You've always been the prize around here."

"What's going on?" Mom poked her head in. That was a surprise. Usually when Tasha and I fought, she turned up the volume on the TV.

"Nothing new," I said. "Tasha's nominating me for Citizen of the Year."

Mom turned on Tasha. "Stop nagging him. Jessica's in the hospital, for God's sake. He must be exhausted."

"So now *I'm* the bad guy. What's new?" Tasha stalked out of the room.

I sighed. "You don't need to keep defending me, Mom. I can handle Tasha."

"She doesn't know when to stop. Never has." Mom turned to leave.

"Wait." I took a deep breath. "She told me about Dad."

Mom nodded. I guess Tasha had already mentioned it. "I did the best I could for you, Darren. I wanted you to have someone to look up to so you wouldn't get into trouble."

I had to laugh. "How'd that work for you?"

"It worked good." She came over and sat on the edge of the bed. "You never got into drugs, did you?"

"'Course not. I'm not dumb enough to start using."

She stiffened. "Your father wasn't dumb either."

"I wouldn't know."

She was silent for a while, and I could tell she was debating whether to say something. "It wasn't all his fault, you know. It was the business he was in. Everyone in the music scene was on something."

That threw me off. "The music scene?"

"Yeah. He used to MC at clubs and parties and all that."

I couldn't believe my dad had been into music. "Why didn't you tell me any of this?"

"Because that whole scene is trouble. When your dad started using, he was just having fun. Never had to pay for his own booze, crack, nothing. He couldn't handle the temptation."

So much about my mom finally clicked. This was why she never wanted me involved in music. "Don't worry, Mom. That would never happen to me. I see what drugs do to people."

"Good."

Mom knew what I was getting at—being a street dealer was a wake-up call for anyone tempted to start using.

Maybe that was why she didn't stop me from dealing. I wasn't going to ask.

The Game

She'll use you
She'll seduce you
Red carpet of cash under your feet
Sure there's guns
Sure there's death
You think you're strong, you take the heat
It's about the ca-ching
The glitter of bling
Only problem is
If you live this biz
You rock the lifestyle
And make big plans
Then you look in the mirror
There's blood on your hands.

THE INTERROGATION

Ray-go was a natural businessman. When we did cash drops together, I let him do the talking. He knew what to say to put the jumpy shop owners at ease.

Sometimes I felt like we were in an old gangster movie. The owners would meet us at the back of their stores and bring us inside for the cash. Most of them didn't want to be involved with Tony, but they were too scared to speak up. Even though he gave them a decent cut of the money, it didn't make up for the worry of getting caught.

We finished the cash drops around nine. It was too late to see Jessica. Since she'd been moved out of ICU, I had to stick to regular visiting hours. I went home, hoping that I wouldn't get a call from one of the executives that night. But it was hard to relax knowing that any day now Tony could give the go-ahead for the Blood bath.

The phone rang. I jumped and grabbed my cell.

But it was the wrong phone.

I scrambled to dig the cell from under my mattress. "Hello?"

"Darren, I'm glad I caught you," Kessler said. "We found the gun at Tyrell's place."

"Is it the murder weapon?"

"Looks like it. The ballistics won't come back for a few days. We've got him here. He's keeping his mouth shut. I want you to come in and watch us question him. Maybe you can help us figure out what will get him talking."

Sounded like her optimism of the other night had taken a hit. I wasn't sure there was anything I could do to help, but I'd try.

"I'm there," I promised, hanging up.

I took a train downtown and scoped the street before slipping into the police station. Kessler met me right away and brought me to Homicide on the second floor, then to an interrogation room with a small black-and-white TV. On it, there was Tyrell, staring down at a table. A bald detective sat next to the TV, writing down notes.

"Detective Reitz, this is Prescott's CI."

"Hello." His eyes were cold, and he didn't shake my hand. I knew what he was thinking—a snitch is a snitch.

"Tyrell hasn't said anything so far but 'Fuck you,'" Reitz said. "Kessler here thinks you might have a strategy to deal with that."

I watched Tyrell on the screen, noticed the way he hung his head, fidgeted nervously with his hands, and shuffled his feet. He was scared. I knew the feeling. I'd never forget the night Vinny had brought me to see Tony, when I'd expected to die.

I turned to Kessler. "He's terrified of Tony. He disobeyed him by keeping the gun. You should play on that. Remind him that he must've gone against Tony's orders and that Tony's gonna be mad. Tell him that Tony won't risk him talking. Tell him he's dead even if he doesn't rat him out."

Kessler and Reitz glanced at each other. Reitz actually said, "Thank you," as he got up. They headed for the door.

"One more thing," I said, and they both turned.

"Remind him that he's got kids. And that for Tony, no one is off-limits."

THE CHINA PLACE

Midnight. I was still at Homicide, my head in my hands.

I'd watched Kessler and Reitz play it as best they could, but it wasn't enough. Tyrell wasn't going to talk. Despite the fear in his eyes, despite his fiendlike jitters, he wasn't going to implicate Tony.

My phone went off for the second time in twenty minutes. Vinny. I'd ignored his last call, but this time I had to take it. I didn't need him getting suspicious.

"Yo."

"Darren, I been calling you. Where you at?"

"Just got home."

"We're about to have a meeting. Nine-one-one, son. Nine-one-one. The China place." He hung up.

So they'd heard that Tyrell had been arrested.

I glanced at the TV screen. I doubted anything would change while I was gone. Kessler and Reitz would probably throw in the towel soon.

The China place was an abandoned town house in a seedy part of Chinatown. The front steps were crumbling, but the back entrance was usable. I'd been here once before. There was no furniture, just dirt and dust and whatever trash the latest squatters had left behind. I watched where I stepped in case there were syringes on the floor.

Inside, everybody was standing in a circle.

"You heard about Tyrell getting picked up?" Vinny asked.

I acted surprised. "When did it happen?"

"Few hours ago."

"What they got on him?"

"We don't know yet," Marcus said.

Tony cracked his knuckles. "Bitch-ass kept a gun I told him to throw away. I'll fuck him up."

"He won't talk, will he?" I asked.

"Nah, he won't talk," Marcus said.

Tony didn't seem so sure. "No doubt the cops will wanna make him a deal."

"It's on him," Vinny said. "It's all on him. You got no worries."

"Don't I? I should've ended him when he fucked up the Blood bath!"

"You couldn't have known this would happen," Marcus said, trying to calm him down. "Tyrell won't snitch. Not if he wants to live another day."

I had a strong instinct on how to play this. "I hope you're right," I said to Marcus. "But the cops will mess with his head. I bet they're telling him that Tony's gonna kill him no matter what, just to make sure he stays quiet."

Marcus glared at me. He wanted to stop Tony from doing something rash.

"Darren's right," Tony said. "Tyrell could talk either way."

"Unless we get him a message that if he keeps his trap shut, you're cool with him," I told Tony.

"Makes sense to me," Ray-go said. "We could send somebody to see him. Let him know that if he stays quiet, we've got his back."

Marcus thought about it. "Maybe McFadden."

Damn it. McFadden was Tony's expensive lawyer. It made perfect sense for him to deliver the message.

Tony shook his head. "This is too steep for him. This ain't some trafficking case. This is about a cop. We can't trust some crooked-ass lawyer with that."

Marcus gave up the point. "Then one of us better do it."

At that moment, we all looked away from Tony.

"Darren," Tony said. "It was your idea. You do it."

"But—" Seeing Tony's hard stare, I nodded grudgingly. "Okay."

My fists tightened with satisfaction. For once, Tony had played right into my hands.

THE MESSENGER

When I got back to the station, it was one in the morning. Kessler was still there. She rubbed her temples like she was fighting a headache. "We couldn't get a word out of him. Not one word. We told him we were picking up his cousin. He didn't flinch."

"Where is he now?"

"In Central Holding downstairs."

"With other guys?"

"Yeah."

"Good. That'll keep him on edge."

"You were right about him, Darren. He's been well programmed. Walker knows how to choose his people."

"I want to see him."

She frowned. "Why?"

"I'm bringing him a message from Diamond Tony. I'll pay off a guard to let me talk to him. Happens all the time."

She didn't deny that. Everybody knew some of the guards took bribes. It was part of the game.

"Maybe it's safer if we make it look like you got picked up," she said.

"No. Tony sent me to deliver a message, and I know exactly what I've got to do. Trust me. It's our last chance."

"Go for it, then."

Minutes later, a guard ushered me up to the cell. Tyrell was in there with four other guys. Most of them were strung out. Tyrell was slumped in a corner, keeping his distance from the others. When he saw me, his eyes bugged out, and he jumped to his feet.

"D." He gripped the bars. "How's Tony?"

He searched my eyes, trying to gauge how much trouble he was in. For a second, I almost felt sorry for him. Then I thought of Prescott.

"He wanted me to give you a message: *You know the code.*"

"'Course I know the code. Ain't nothing they can do to make me talk. Remy neither. Tony knows that, right?"

I looked away, knowing that what you didn't say could be heavier than what you did. "I'm just the messenger. That's all he said." I started to walk away, but Tyrell grabbed my sleeve through the bars. The guard in the hall barked for him to back off, so he let go.

"You gotta tell Tony he can trust me." His voice shook. "You gotta tell him. I know it was a big mistake to keep the gun, but it was too good to throw away. I was gonna use it for—*you* know. It don't jam, see. I needed a piece like that. One I could depend on."

I shrugged. "I'll tell him if you want."

"The cops are saying he's gonna kill me either way. But I know that ain't true. Tony trusts me."

He was begging me to say something to reassure him, but I gave him nothing. I wouldn't even look at him.

"Good luck, T." I knocked his knuckles through the bars, then walked away.

The Snitch's Dilemma

Every man will have his chance
To place his final bet
Stick to your story, Morning Glory
Cut a deal, slip from the net

TAKEDOWN

Betray the King and then survive
It might be the only way
To save your family and yourself
Go with your gut and make the play.

ICE COLD

That night, I slept like a baby. And when I woke up, the secret cell was ringing.

"Tyrell's talking," Kessler said. "Whatever you did worked."

I closed my eyes and breathed deeply. This wasn't a dream. Diamond Tony was going to get put away for Prescott's murder. Finally he would get what he deserved.

"I'd like to pick up Walker as soon as possible," she said. "Word could get out that Tyrell talked, and I don't want Tony skipping town. Can you locate him for me?"

I checked the clock. It was 9:05 a.m. "He's probably still at his crib. I think only Marcus knows where it is. Odds are Tony's going to want to meet with his executives at some point today. I'll keep you posted."

"I'll be waiting for your call. And, Darren—thank you. Ed was right about you. You're a good kid."

"Thank me once Tony's locked up." I didn't feel much like a kid anymore. Hadn't for a long time.

Less than an hour later, I walked into the China place. Only Tony and Marcus were there. Tony paced the room like a restless cat.

When he saw me, he took off his sunglasses. His eyes were red, as if he hadn't slept. "Tell me about your meeting with Tyrell."

Obviously the text I'd sent Tony last night hadn't reassured him. That suited me just fine. I'd called Kessler minutes ago with our location. The cops would be here any second.

"I told him everything you wanted me to. He knows he's dead if he opens his mouth."

My pulse was going crazy, but by now I'd learned to appear ice cold no matter what was going on inside me. I kept expecting the door to get kicked in at any moment. I was ready to hit the floor with my hands behind my back.

"He wanted me to tell you that he's no snitch," I said.

Tony stopped pacing. "I bet they're leaning on him hard."

I spread my hands. "I told him you'd have his back and take care of his family if he kept quiet. But he was stressed out. I can't tell you a hundred percent that we can count on him. I don't know."

Tony's jaw flexed. "We can't have him talking." He flashed Marcus a look. "You got someone?"

Marcus gave a nod. "I have a couple of possibilities."

"*Possibilities?* I need someone who can do the job and not fuck it up. You got someone or not?"

"Yeah. When do you want it done?"

"Yesterday."

Marcus got on his phone.

Holy shit. Tony really wasn't going to take any chances. I guess I'd done Tyrell a favor by getting him to talk. If he hadn't been transferred out of the city yet, it would have to happen right away. I'd tell Kessler as soon as I got out of here.

Where the hell were the police, anyway?

Tony was muttering—to me or to himself, I wasn't sure. "I wanted one job done, one easy job. Now I have to deal with fuckups like Tyrell. I'm not going down. No way I'm going down."

"Tyrell will be out of the picture soon," I assured him. "Marcus is on it."

"He might've already talked. They could have a taped confession by now!"

"I don't know how it works, but if he can't testify in court—"

"*Cops! Cops!*"

The shouts came from the back porch. Ashtray ran in. "We spotted the cops a block down. Get out—now!"

RUN

Tony pulled a gun from under his shirt. "Get back out there," he ordered Ashtray. "Keep them away from the house."

Ashtray looked panicked, but he followed orders.

Tony and Marcus didn't hesitate. They bolted upstairs. I went with them, though I had no idea where they were going. I'd have thought they'd make a break out the back before the place got surrounded.

Tony headed for a bedroom cluttered with broken furniture. He tore open a closet door and disappeared inside. Marcus went after him. I stared into the closet. There was a hole in the wall that led into another room.

Into another apartment, I realized. The houses were connected. I crawled through.

"Close the closet!" Tony shouted back to me. We were in another abandoned house. Tony and Marcus ran down a hallway, then crossed to another house through another hole in a bedroom wall.

As I ran with them, my mind reeled. Tony had this escape route planned. That was why we'd met in this building in the first place.

Paranoia paid off.

In the third house, we ran downstairs to the back door. Marcus peered out the dirty, half-broken window. We heard gunshots. Ashtray and the other security guys must have been following Tony's orders and firing their guns to keep the cops away from the house.

"We clear?" Tony demanded.

"There's a lot of them out there," Marcus said, trying to catch his breath. "We should wait till they take the house. If most of them go inside, we've got a better chance of getting away."

Tony pushed him aside and looked out the window himself. "We go *now*. If we wait for them to get inside the house, we'll only have a few minutes till they track us here. You go first," he said to Marcus. "Stay low to those bushes. You'll make it."

Marcus opened his mouth to argue, but his gaze flicked down to Tony's gun. "Okay."

Marcus slipped outside, crouching low. Tony and I watched from the window as he hid behind some bushes ten feet from the house. Police were all over the place. There was no way I could go out there—the odds of getting shot were too high. The cops wouldn't know I was on their side. To them, I was just another of Tony Walker's crew.

A cop suddenly called to the others and waved them over. He'd spotted Marcus in the bushes. Marcus made a break for it.

"Freeze!" several cops shouted.

Marcus didn't stop. He ran at full speed, firing on the cops. They returned fire.

"Now!" Tony grabbed my arm and shoved me outside. Bastard wanted me to eat the bullets while he slipped away.

Fuck him.

I tried to push back inside, but Tony blocked the doorway. "I said, *Go now.* I'll stay close."

"It's suicide," I said. "We're better off letting them take us in."

The shooting stopped. I glanced over my shoulder and saw that Marcus was down. When I turned back, I found myself staring into the barrel of Tony's gun. "We go together, or I drop you right now."

I didn't move. "I'm not taking bullets for you. You're on your own."

Tony's eyes were easy to read. He was going to squeeze the trigger.

I lunged, head butting him in the face. I grabbed for his gun just as it went off. Bullets whizzed past me. I'd barely registered the slice of pain in my neck when Tony tried to shove me to the ground. Catching him in a bear hug, we went flying down the steps.

My head made contact with the pavement, and dark spots flashed in front of my eyes. Tony scrambled to his feet and broke into a run.

I lifted my head to see him shooting the air full of bullets. The cops shot back. Tony took a bullet in the shoulder, but kept going. The next bullet caught his head, and I had to look away—but not before I saw blood and bits of skull explode. He fell to the ground.

It was getting harder and harder to breathe. My neck burned. When I reached up to touch it, my hand came away covered in blood.

And then my world went black.

SUNRISE

I woke up to Kiki jumping on my bed and giggling.

"Can't I sleep a few more minutes?"

"No!" He clapped his hands on my ears. "No! No! No!"

I couldn't help laughing. "How about we go eat breakfast?"

"No! No! No!"

But he dissolved in laughter when I Superman-carried him into the kitchen and plunked him down in his booster seat.

Tasha already had his Cheerios and banana slices ready.

"Where'd you go last night?" she asked. It didn't sound like an accusation, but you never knew with Tasha.

"Jessica's dad made dinner. It was ridiculous. The man's an Iron Chef."

"Lucky you. How's Jessica doing, anyway?"

"Better every day. She's back at school." Jessica's determination blew me away. She was already caught up and achieving top marks, though physically she still had to take it easy. She was even talking about a summer co-op placement.

"That's great." Tasha paused, as if she wanted to say more on that, but then said, "I'm out of class early today, so if you want me to pick up Kiki . . ."

"I got it. Right, Kiki?"

He gave me a sticky high five.

Tasha was nicer these days. It was weird. Now that I was around a lot more, she'd run out of reasons to bitch at me. Maybe that would change, but for now, it was a relief.

Both she and Mom knew I was out of the biz. The whole neighborhood had heard what happened to Diamond Tony, Marcus, and me that day. But nobody knew that the bullet that grazed my neck was from Tony's gun, and nobody ever would.

There were no more cash drops on the kitchen table. Mom never said a word about it. Her dream of living large might be dead, but I knew she was glad I wasn't dead too.

Since Tony's death, everything had changed. The moment

Andre got released, he'd taken back the streets. He'd shattered what was left of Diamond Tony's operation, secured his old suppliers, and kept a tight rein on his dealers. I'd gotten out just in time.

I took a shower, then headed out to pick up my choco-latte. The moment I got to the bus stop, Trey launched into the weather forecast for the rest of the week. Sunshine all the way. I sipped my drink and smiled.

"Our bus!" Trey cheered. "I knew it was going to be early today."

"You called it."

Trey started to reply, but I wasn't listening. A car was parked a few yards away with two guys in hoodies in the front seat. My instincts prickled. They were watching me.

The guy in the passenger seat got out and walked toward me, his eyes deadlocked with mine. The bus pulled up to the curb, its brakes making a long squeak before the doors opened.

Trey got on. The guy in the hoodie was just ten feet from me, hands in his pockets. He was turned away from the bus, as if he didn't want anyone to see his face.

"Darren, you coming?" Trey shouted.

I was tempted to hurl myself onto the bus. But I couldn't do it. If this was it—if I was going to get shot—I didn't want anyone else getting hit too. I took a breath and shook my head. "Nah, I'll get the next one." The door closed in front of Trey's puzzled face, and the bus pulled away.

"Darren." The guy pushed his hood back. He was older than me, maybe twenty-five, with sharp brown eyes and a slight dent in the side of his skull, like he'd taken a bullet there. "Darren Lewis."

"That's my name." I broke eye contact for a split second, scanning for an escape route. There wasn't one.

"You were one of Tony Walker's executives."

"Once upon a time."

"I want to thank you. And make you an offer."

Suddenly I knew who he was. The bloodred ruby in his left ear gave him away. "Andre."

"Yeah." He smiled. "Enjoying my freedom."

Was he ever. The streets were his now.

"I understand you're an effective infiltrator," he said.

I didn't react. Didn't even flinch.

"My lawyer heard the cops had a CI inside Walker's operation," he said. "I figured that might be you."

"How'd you figure that?"

"You survived. When Tony and Marcus were shot dead, you lived. And then you got out of the game."

He'd guessed the truth. Made it sound so damned easy. "You got it wrong."

"Whatever you say. I came here to ask you to work for me. I could use someone connected to Walker's old crew. Rumor has it Ray-go is trying a little start-up operation."

The news caught me off guard, but it shouldn't have. Ray-go had the ambition and the connections to go into business for himself. Andre was right to be concerned.

"I'm not interested," I said.

"You can name your pay."

"I'm out. For good."

He looked skeptical. "I said that once too. Problem is, the game is like the product we sell. Once it's in your blood, you need it to feel alive."

"Not me." I wasn't like the others. I didn't need the status, the money, the adrenaline. What I needed was to start over.

"I'll take your word for it."

Andre could force the issue if he wanted to. He knew the truth about me, and that could still get me killed any day of the week. But instead, he slipped something into my hand. It felt like a wad of cash. "Enjoy your new life, Darren."

Before I could reply or hand him back the cash, he went to his car and got inside. The car started up and made a U-turn.

I glanced down at the money in my hand. It was a couple of grand at least. I hoped it was just a thank-you. I hoped I'd never see him again. But I had the feeling that if Andre needed something, I'd be hearing from him.

A gust of wind hit me. I looked back, watching until the car was out of sight. Maybe I was just being paranoid. But that's the thing about the game. If you weren't paranoid, you were dead already.

ACKNOWLEDGMENTS

To the pros:

John Rudolph, my agent, for believing in Darren's story, and in me. My editor, Annette Pollert, for making this a better book. And the Ontario Arts Council for its generous support.

To my peeps:

My family, for their support, and for their patience when I have a deadline. My friends, the ones who call me Al. And my writer pals, especially Debbie Mason.

ABOUT THE AUTHOR

Allison van Diepen is also the author of *Street Pharm, Snitch, Raven,* and *The Vampire Stalker.* She teaches at an alternative high school in Ottawa, Canada. Visit her at AllisonvanDiepen.com.